"*Girl, World* had me gripped from the very first page, and many of its voices will stay with me for a very long time; all of them are deserving of a novel of their own, in fact! This fascinating, edgy, and accomplished collection often draws on the author's own experiences in some of the most troubled parts of the world and even when she throws her characters into the most awful situations, she has a talent for finding humour, energy and, sometimes, rays of hope. *Girl, World* illuminates the experience of young women today in ways that are by turns surprising, funny, and devastating. Poppe is a writer to watch."

Zoe Strachan, author of *Negative Space*,
winner of the Betty Trask award

"Alex Poppe, trained as an actress, gave up her career and in a courageous move few Western women would dare to make, went alone to Iraq to become a teacher, fulfilled a dream and became a writer. Her story is inspiring and her talent is clear and her writing is bold and vivid. Her work is about women and what it is like to be a woman, but only partially, for her work is much more about the vast, nervous, unsettled world from the Balkans to Kurdistan to New York. She is a writer with the eye of a journalist whose prose is bold, unique, unsparing, and vivid. Her stories can be hard to read, but the reader knows they are true and that is why they are good. She is a writer on her way and one to watch."

Jere Van Dyk, Journalist,
CBS News, author of Captive

"Since the dawn of the Digital Revolution, facts have fallen into disrepute. They're too contradictory, too refutable, too malleable. Histories too have fallen into disfavor, a mere thesis feeling unequal to the complex ambiguities of our times. It is the fiction writers who have been filling this vacuum, wanting to capture the essence, often the essential horror, of a time and place. Above all, perhaps, is Land of Green Plums, what history could depict Müller's portrait of Ceausescu's Romania. But more recently we have seen Englander's Argentina and Marra's Chechnya. Now here comes Alex Poppe's debut collection, Girl, World, with its similar ambitions. A panoramic view of women's lives from the sex-trafficking gulags to Kurdistan, from the rape victims to social media Islam, this is a searing collection of up-to-the-second stories. Unsentimental, driven by sparking kinetic language, Poppe swaps backgrounds while never losing sight of the essence of what it means to be a woman in the second decade of our new century. She is generous to the reader, there is nothing polemical here, just searing honest snapshots of courage against horrendous odds."

Joel Hinman, Editor-at-Large,
Epiphany Magazine

Girl, World

stories by Alex poppe

Laughing *Fire*
press

Copyright © 2016 Alex Poppe

All rights reserved. No part of this book may be reproduced in any form or by any electronic or mechanical means including informational storage and retrieval systems without written permission from the publisher, except by a reviewer, who may quote brief passages in a review.

ISBN 978-0-9964905-5-9

www.laughingfire.com

For H
always and forever

Acknowledgements

Acknowledgements are due to the editors of the following publications where earlier versions of these stories first appeared. "Family Matter" was first published by the *Massachusetts Review*. "Moxie" was first published by the *Tacoma Literary Review*, with a special shout out to its publisher Joe Ponepinto whose enthusiasm for my words helped buoy my spirits during those days when I felt as if I couldn't write anything worth reading. "The Crystal Fairies" was a semi-finalist for the *Conium Review*'s Innovative Short Fiction Prize and was ultimately published by *Stoneboat Literary Journal*. "Kurdistan" was a finalist in *Glimmer Train*'s Family Matter Contest and was published by *Prick of the Spindle*, as was "My Mother's Daughter". "Room 308" was published by the *Laurel Review*. The *Laurel Review* also nominated this story for a Pushcart Prize. Across the pond in the UK, "V" was published by *SHORT FICTION, the visual literary journal* while "Ras Al-Amud" was published by *Litro*.

Everything I know about writing comes from The Writers Studio, NY. My editing skills were sharpened while earning my Master's degree at the University of Glasgow. Thanks to the teachers and workshop partners at those institutions. Therese Eiben and Zoe Strachan, thank you for so much support.

Special thanks to Tony Clerkson, who workshopped most of this collection and whose comments made sure every word counted. Thanks to Annika Kaiser, Gwen Davies and Karen Emslie who offered critiques on various stories. Thanks to Ian McDonald who supportively read my writing when I was just starting out and it was the absolute last thing he wanted to do, and to Holger Seidel, who is the ultimate proofreader.

I couldn't have written this collection without knowing the wonderful people who populate it. John Fico, "Family Matter" is my love letter to our friendship. Camren Parrish, the best parts of Frieda were born in you. Thank you to all my wonderful students whose lives have influenced my writing, especially my lovely students at the International School of Choueifat, Erbil and AMIDEAST in Jerusalem. "Kurdistan" and "Ras Al-Amud" would not exist without you.

Finally, thanks to my mother and father, for without them, none of this would be possible.

Girl, World

My Mother's Daughter	1
V	9
Room 308	33
Moxie	51
Kurdistan	85
Ras Al-Amud	112
The Crystal Fairies	125
Family Matter	139

My Mother's Daughter

Help Wanted

In the truck we were mostly virgins. We had long slender torsos and still longer legs and manicured nails. Some of us were on the cusp of adulthood having just graduated high school and some of us still needed looking after. Some of us came from the great city of Schevchenko but grew up looking westward, longing for Levi's. Many more of us came from the heartland and didn't look past that year's harvest, which had stopped growing. Some of us came from the coastline, having birthday *shasliks* along the Black Sea. Some of us came from the mountains that separated sister satellite states during the Cold War. We had watched our fathers and uncles and brothers cross and crisscross those mountains and fade into the horizon. Now it was time for us to be on our way.

In the truck the first thing we did – before we shared our names or silently judged who was wearing too much makeup or decided which one was the prettiest – was compare our upcoming jobs. Some of us were to be au pairs living in mansions and some of us were to be waitresses in five star restaurants. *My aunt's husband arranged it. He has a color TV and his own stereo system.* More of us were to be maids in fancy resorts. Some of us held bended business cards with contact names in fancy lettering Some of us clutched dogeared

GIRL, WORLD

pamphlets showing smiling young women in smart maids' uniforms, smiling young women serving platters of food we couldn't have consumed in a week, smiling young women pushing prams in parks. *You won't even think of it as work.* These were jobs our mothers and sisters and aunts had back home, but no one smiled with all her teeth when she did them.

In the truck some of us thought fondly of the mother's cheeks we had kissed goodbye before embarking on our big adventure. *I promise to write just as soon as I can.* Some of us felt guilty about sneaking off in the middle of the night, leaving only a scribbled note of explanation. *I had to. She wouldn't have let me go otherwise.* Some of us looked back through tears of second thoughts and some of us looked forward to promises of better times. One of us held hands with a lifelong best friend we had convinced to come with us instead of taking a job making Xerox copies after graduation. *This is the best decision you have ever made!*

In the truck we wondered about our futures. Would the jobs be hard? Would we make friends? Would we fall in love and stay forever?

We dreamt of being on our own for the first time. We dreamt of modern new apartments with wall-to-wall carpeting and built-in shower stall bathrooms and ice cube making refrigerators. We saw ourselves drinking Coca-Cola whenever we wanted some. We dreamt of McDonald's French fries for dinner and Snickers bars for breakfast. We dreamt of buying clothes in shops with dressing rooms instead buying them from babushkas standing behind tables outside the metro station. We dreamt of selection. We dreamt of real Nike tennis shoes. We dreamt of houses not owned by the government but by ourselves and our husbands, who would worship us. We dreamt of daughters whose favorite bedtime

ALEX POPPE

story would be "When Mama First Left Home".

WHAT WAS TAKEN

We each took one suitcase. Some of us packed swimsuits that would have made our grandmothers blush. Some of us packed rosaries that used to be hidden under heavy sweaters in the top right bureau drawer. Some of us packed single tins of homemade honey cookies and ate them when we thought no one was looking. All of us packed high heels and one petite girl packed pale pink toe shoes too. In our bags there were hair ribbons and nail polish and colored pencils. Some of us brought sketch books and some of us brought diaries. No one brought an English phrase book. Everyone took exactly one good dress. *I wore this to my sister's wedding.* Everyone packed makeup. Everyone packed dime-store rhinestone jewelry. Everyone packed synthetic polyester undergarments. Not all of us yet needed bras. One of us forgot her toothbrush but remembered her stuffed teddy bear with the missing left ear. All of us took for granted the driver holding our identity papers.

As night fell, we took turns guessing why the drivers changed along the roads and which direction we were headed. Some of us insisted all was well. Some of us voiced doubts. All of us wanted to use a bathroom. None of us were brave enough to ask. We took turns guessing how much farther. We took turns singing our village songs. When the driver shouted at us to be quiet, we took turns staring at each other in silence. Some of us twirled our hair around our fingers. Some of us patted another's arm. One of us folded her hands and prayed silently. All of us took shallow breaths. When the truck rolled to a stop, we took turns thanking God and cursing the driver.

GIRL, WORLD

At that point we had no idea where we had been taken to. At that point we had no idea that we had been taken, too.

Out of the truck some of us wished we had taken warmer clothes. Out of the truck some of us stretched our legs and pretended not to notice a large roll of bills being handed to the driver by a man no one had seen before. Out of the truck some of us wondered why we and our suitcases were being left in the middle of nowhere. Out of the truck all of us suddenly wanted the cursed driver not to drive away. Out of the truck all of us drew into a tight huddle surrounded by more men we had never seen before. Out of the truck some of us noticed their guns tucked into their waistbands. Out of the truck no one moved when they ordered us to strip. Out of the truck all of us saw them remove their guns from their waistbands. Out of the truck one of us removed her dress. Then another one removed her shirt. Then a man tore off another's skirt. Another man pulled a girl by her hair and ripped down her trousers. Another man slapped a statue-still red-haired girl *hard* across her face making a red welt. He slapped her again and again and still she did not move. He put his gun to her temple. She did not move. Then he pulled the trigger. Some of us wiped splattered blood from our shoulders and cheeks. Some of us tasted acrid iron in our mouths. Some of us shed silent tears. The rest of us shed our remaining clothes.

BREAKING GROUND

They bought us and then they broke us. They broke us nonchalantly. They broke us cruelly. They broke us robotically, but thoroughly while making jokes. They laughed at us who were virgins when they broke through. *I'm her first.* They broke us hesitantly. *Aw, he's shy. It must be his first.* They broke us

ALEX POPPE

quickly. They broke us slowly to build up fear. They broke us singularly. They broke us in groups. They had contests to see who could break more. They took turns. If they liked us, they broke us again. And again. And again. *My girlfriend.* They broke us face down in a dirt courtyard with moist mud in our mouths. They broke us face up blinded by the sun in our eyes. They broke us where the other girls could see. They broke us from behind so we couldn't see. They broke us against a chain link fence that broke our freedom. They broke our nails so we couldn't scratch. They broke our skin with their cigarettes. A fourteen-year-old girl, they broke her neck. *Let this be a lesson if you try to run.* They broke us pulled half asleep from makeshift beds. They broke us till we bled. They broke us so we could never be put back together again.

They broke us held down on crumb strewn table tops with bottles. They broke us bent over wooden benches with bottles. They broke us on hands and bended knees with fists and bottles. They broke us by the heel of their combat boots, blue UN baseball caps firmly planted on their heads. They broke us until there was nothing that could be said. *I hope my mother believes me dead.* They broke us to the sound of birds singing. They broke us as a mid-morning coffee break when there was no coffee. They broke us for sport. They broke us to pass the time. They broke us between card games. They broke us silhouetted in moonlight. They broke us in the blackest of night. When dawn broke, they broke us anew. They *broke* us. Then they sold us.

HOME LIFE

We were sold to the brothels that multiplied along the Bosnian hillside when the war ended and the peacekeepers came.

GIRL, WORLD

Home was a bare mattress behind a locked-from-the-outside door of a hidden pantry at the Nightclub Florida. Home was a shared bunk in an overcrowded room adjacent to Mississippi Madness. Home was a rotating cot above Texas Dance. Home was a spot on the floor in a storage shed behind Big Ben's Social Club. For those who tried to run away, home was the river bed of the River Bosna.

At home, they watched us from sunup to sundown. They watched us through a peep hole while we slept. They watched us in the shower to make sure we did not slit our wrists. They watched us at meal time to make sure we ate, but not too much. One of us they made into one of them. She watched us for signs of trouble. For a reduced freedom price, she made sure we put on makeup and high heels and bright smiles before we entered the clubs. Then she put on her own makeup and high heels and bright smile and silently followed.

In the clubs we donned our costumes and danced on bar tops for UN peacekeepers, on table tops for Bosnian policemen, on the laps of DynCorp security personnel. We drank champagne with the peacekeepers. We drank Russian vodka with the police. Security liked their whisky and rye. And when the bottles were empty, we danced naked on our backs in rooms rented by the hour to pay off our ever compounding debts. We owed for our buying price. *I can't believe I am worth that much.* We owed for our travel, so far from our homelands. We owed for food, water, and shelter. We owed for the dance costumes that neither we nor the customers wanted us to wear. If one of us ran off, we owed for her debts too.

Some of us would dance five or six times a night. *I get as drunk as I can so I don't feel a thing.* Some of us refused to dance and would be locked in a closet for days at a time without food. *At least I get a break from the sex.* Some of

ALEX POPPE

us preferred the UN peacekeepers. *Dennis says he'll pay my debt before he leaves the country.* None of us believed that would happen. Some of us preferred the Bosnians. *At least I can understand some of what they are saying.* None of us preferred the DynCorp security personnel. *They're rough pigs!* Some of us forgot every face as soon as he rolled off. Some of us had every face forever etched into our minds. We would spend a lifetime unable to forget. Some of us had regulars. If our regulars were high ranking, we gained a bit of protection. *Careful with this one. She's General Klein's girl.* Some of us received small gifts. *Thank you for the Milky Way bars Deputy Commissioner.* Some of us received small indispositions. *God these fever blisters burn.* Some of us received big indispositions, which if not taken care of in the first trimester whether we wanted to or not, were eventually revealed. When some of us undeniably showed, the problem would disappear, and so would we.

When there were private parties all of us in the brothel worked. When there were private parties all of us in the brothel were well fed. When there were private parties there weren't enough beds. Customers would take two or more of us at a time. *He thinks he's a sultan.* When there were private parties everybody drank too much. When there were private parties everybody fought too much. When there were private parties everybody cocked his pistol. Some of us became protective shields. Some of us became bargaining chips. A few of us became peace offerings. We'd silently curse or pray until the guns were put away.

When there were private parties the "nightclubs" opened late the next day. When there were private parties all of us spent the next day on hands and knees. We cleaned puke from club floors, puke from urinals, puke from under our fingernails.

GIRL, WORLD

We tended to soreness and swelling and bruises. We'd gently wash each other's cuts. And as we sang half remembered lull-la-byes, we'd hold our mattresses up from the floor and tally another day's score onto the concrete core below. *781 more tricks and I'm free!*

V

The symbol of Kurdish hope flashes her "V" for victory sign in a photo that goes viral. She has killed a hundred ISIS militants outside Kobani, and now she is hot, hot, hot. Her pseudonym is Rehana and her sisters-in-arms have been trading kitchen cutlery for Kalashnikovs ever since Chemical Ali chased the Kurds up the hill with his toxoid apple gas.

Sabiha Sahar, in the computer room of the Oakland Public Library, peers at the photo so closely her nose touches the screen. Her heavy hair grapevines the keyboard. Rehana's not just about defending the Kurdish homeland: she fought to keep women from being locked in their houses, for Chrissake – just what Sabiha craves. She thinks they should have been sisters, thousands of miles and another world apart. At least she'd know the basics of star navigation or how to shoot a gun. Sabiha is a caged bird who wants her home to be the sky.

The ten thousand strong female battalion, the Peshmergettes, she reads, has a female chain of command, including its own chief. In the photo, Rehana wears matching camouflage pants and shirt, her hips neatly defined by an ammo belt. An upside down middle finger salute steadies the rifle at her side. She looks like a sexy GI Jane doll, her streaked blond hair loosely braided down her back. Sabiha wears a baggy black shirt over a shapeless long black skirt. While

GIRL, WORLD

she reads, her nimble fingers weave her hair. When the braid is finished, Sabiha stares past Rehana, at the edges of her, to blur Rehana's face so their in-commons become keener.

In her mind's eye, Sabiha unbuttons the camouflage shirt and sees plastic-doll smooth skin. She buffs the light tan color with the pad of her thumb until Rehana gleams alabaster. White girls get to do more than brown girls, but no girl gets to do more than a boy. Boys are always on top, right? So there's always a problem if you're the kind of girl who wants to do stuff. Sabiha wants to do *a lot* of stuff, all at the same time, but she doesn't know what exactly, which sidelines her eager self.

Sabiha reads on. In the nineteenth century, Kara Fatma led a battalion of seven hundred men in the Ottoman Empire and stuck forty-three women into the army ranks. It's the twenty-first century and Sabiha's brother doesn't let her wear makeup to high school. She keeps Wet Ones in her book bag so she can wipe it off before she takes the afternoon bus. Let's not talk about the skinny jeans she hides in her school locker.

The dead-leaf crinkle of tinfoil scratches her ear. A girl in a gray hijab and chador coughs as she finishes unwrapping a sandwich hidden in her lap. A petticoat of lettuce swirls around the edges. Sabiha hits control/print and saunters to the beat of invisible club music to the front of the room. She positions herself in the sight line between Hijab and Chador and the computer room supervisor and strikes a pose. Hijab and Chador stares furiously at a half-filled notebook page as her mouth slow-motion chews. The supervisor hands Sabiha her printouts of the Rehana "V" photo and the Peshmergettes, which she safeguards in the side compartment of her bag. Hijab and Chador coughs again, and Sabiha knows she

ALEX POPPE

is balling the foil in her fist, squeezing the day's grievances into its forgiving shape. Outside the library windows, the evening is purpling. Inside Sabiha's head, an electric guitar riffs twice. It sounds like a kaleidoscope of stars. The city bus smells of Fritos and wet socks. Sabiha tucks her nose into her shirt collar and inhales her own girl smell. If her scent were music, it would be the honeyed melody of a Spanish classical guitar flirting in toe shoes with a flute. Out of nowhere, dog-kiss raindrops slather the window panes. The *Black Lives Matter* protestors in Oscar Grant Plaza pop their hoodies or gather under scant awnings in clusters as complex as snowflakes. Sabiha graffities the glass with her fingertip. When she exits, a track of "V"s stand *en pointe* in her wake.

As the wind catches it, the screen door bangs a samba, announcing Sabiha's arrival home. Her mother is making dinner with a phone cradled between her shoulder and ear. Her bones make a step ladder in her chest. When Sabiha hears her mother's swoon song of Kurdish, she knows the phone line stretches to Dubai, where her father spools out affection like kite string. The last time Sabiha spoke to him was seven months, twelve days, and four hours ago. Sabiha beats it to her bedroom.

Sirood enters without knocking. Ever since their father was transferred to The Emirates, her brother thinks it's his God given right to tell her what to do. 'Where were you?' he demands and straddles her desk chair, resting his chalky elbows on its wooden back. Was it only last summer that she filmed his Ice Bucket challenge? He strokes his chin. He's so proud of that newly sprung facial hair.

'It's still there. You can stop touching it.'

'I asked you where you were.'

GIRL, WORLD

Sabiha is Queen of the Dirty Look, which Sirood ignores. Fine. Practice makes perfect. 'The LIE-brary.'

'Sabiha, there are protests everywhere. I worry about you. We may have been born here, but people don't think we belong.'

Sabiha mentally erases the boy-hair dirtying his upper lip, splotchy along his chin. Now Sirood is The Finder of Lost Toys, The Inventor of Games, The Prolonger of Bedtime Stories. She relents. 'I know, but I'm careful. I'm almost fifteen.' She sits up straighter.

'Exactly.' Sirood's voice is dusty.

'Anyway, what do you think Dad wants?'

'What makes you think he wants something? He calls because he misses us.'

'Yeah, that's why he talks to us.' Sabiha reads the fine print of Sirood's face. 'He talked to you?'

'Just for a second. Mostly to remind me to watch out for you.'

Sirood's voice changes to a texture Sabiha can't name: velvet, sandpaper, rain. A lone saxophone wails in her head.

'I can watch out for myself.'

'Okay tough girl. But the tougher ones are easier to hurt.'

Now his voice is a cat weaving around her ankle. She decides not to fight him for the moment. 'Why do you think Dad doesn't want to talk to me?'

Sirood doesn't thrive on tiny cruelties. 'He wants to. You weren't home. He's real busy.'

An ache opens in Sabiha's gut and spreads to her chest. *I'm home now.* 'I don't care.' She turns on her side and curls into a pill bug.

The chair scrapes the bare floor, and then Sirood is sitting on her bed, causing her body to tip slightly towards him. A

ALEX POPPE

hand warms her right shoulder. Sabiha shrugs it off. *They probably talk whenever I'm not around.* The silence they fall into has something hard at the bottom. Rain stamps the rooftop.

*

Jesse is a beefy boy with a Jesus mane men twice his age would kill for. He'll be eighteen in four months and seven days and then it's *fuck this place*! He's joining the Marines and high school won't ever be the same without him. Sabiha watches him from across the lunchroom, watches as he jabs the air with a French fry, talking about getting *hajis*, watches as his arm slips around his girlfriend's twiggy shoulder, disturbing her mermaid hair. His index finger twigs her nipple and a spark flies out and catches Sabiha in the eye, so she doesn't see a table full of faces swivel in her direction. It's only later, when she's settled in the library, does Sabiha realize *haji* was a dog whistle calling everyone to look at her.

Sabiha takes the photos of Rehana and the Peshmergettes out of her book bag. The battalion is a box of Whitman's Sampler with its top off: Rehana is as light as milky tea while some girls are as dark as polished oak. One or two are Jesse-white. Most of the people in the computer room are a Starbucks variety. Since when did Sabiha's world get thrown behind a sepia-toned viewfinder?

The door opens and Hijab and Chador snags on the doorframe before striding towards a trio of empty chairs keeping Sabiha company. The chador's hem sails out behind the girl's denim clad legs and flaps back to kiss her calves. A thought so crazy it seems sane crosses Sabiha's mind: they are destined to be friends.

GIRL, WORLD

Sit here. Sit here. Sit here. Sabiha closes her eyes to focus her inner magnetic pull. When she opens them, Hijab and Chador is lounging one computer away. Sabiha's aim has always been a little off.

Hijab and Chador slants her a look.

Sabiha smiles. This is going to be easier than she thought.

Hijab and Chador seals herself behind an arm wall. She hooks her thumb under her ear to cradle her head and surfs the web. Suddenly, she turns and laser-stares into Sabiha's pupils as if to drill a hole in her skull. 'What do you want?' Hijab and Chador's voice is a brick wall.

What does she want? Sabiha wants to know why her father doesn't speak to her. She wants to know, when you kiss a boy, where the noses go. For just one day, she wants to be one of those girls whose clothes look like they are trying to flee their bodies. She wants her life to start already, and what's takin' it so flipping long. 'What's your name?'

'Hira.' The two syllables come to Sabiha from across a long bridge.

'I'm Sabiha.'

'Great. We done here?' Hira returns her face to her computer screen.

'I–'

Hira doesn't break her typing. 'Just because we're both sand niggers doesn't mean I want to talk you. Now fuck off.'

Sabiha tenses as if freezing water were being dumped down her back. Turning to her computer screen, she draws the curtain of her hair so Hira can't see the magenta scribbling her cheeks. A spiral notebook slaps shut. A zipper rips closed. A chair scrapes away. One, two, three and Hira is gone baby gone. A black and white *keffiyeh* lies forgotten under her desk. Sabiha rescues the scarf and runs out of the

ALEX POPPE

computer room. No Hira in the hallway. No Hira in the lot outside. Sabiha feels the sidewalk pushing through her shoes. It propels her back into the computer room.

The page Hira was looking at features honey-colored pancakes striped insouciant with syrup. Sabiha scrolls through pictures. The next snap frames a white egg lazing in a white square bowl on a '60s psychedelic white and blue flowered background. Then the egg is gone and there is centerfold sugar gleaming white on white. Languid oil follows sugar and then salt takes its turn, lounging in the square bowl. It looks like a pop-art pictorial on how to make pancakes. Sabiha doesn't know the website *Al-Zawra* so she puts some text into Google Translator. "For women who are interested in explosive belt and suicide bombing—"

Right now Sabiha wishes she were under her quilted bedspread listening to Lana Del Rey on her headphones. Then she wouldn't have to think about Hira's head, arms and legs blasting off her body like the rays off a starfish. She wouldn't hear the whirl of helicopters harmonizing with a chorus of sirens. Goosebumps flower her back.

She should tell someone. What if someone already knows? What if the NSA is watching her right now through the library computer? Wait, there's no camera on the monitor. For safety, Sabiha ties Hira's *keffiyeh* around her face, gangsta style. The soft cloth smells of sweat and tuberose.

The Sisterhood of the Caliphate shows girls about Sabiha's age carrying AK47's, teens decorated with grenades. One poster child wears a stethoscope around her neck and a Kalashnikov on her shoulder. There are classes in cooking and sewing and weaponry. The Sisterhood gather like the suburban moms in Rockridge do, minding their kids together on playgrounds. But all work and no play makes Jill a very

GIRL, WORLD

cranky *hausfrau*. These jihadi wives meet for coffee or go to restaurants backlit by sunsets while they wait for their handsome husbands to be martyred in the holy war.

Sabiha twirls a lock of her hair instead of chewing it. The girls in the photos are part of something bigger. They matter. At school, the only girls that matter are the cheerleaders and the half-sluts, and there's a lot of overlap. Jesse will never write on her with his fountain pen ink eyes. His hard/soft mouth will never inch in her direction. She sees herself as her classmates see her, a loner, the dull cream school walls surrounding her like a milk carton. What did Hira call them? Sand niggers. Sabiha has never thought of herself like a – there's no polite way to say it – sand nigger. But, Hira's right. Even Sabiha's father doesn't give her the time of day. She gathers her things. She exits the computer room, lingering in the doorway like a climbing vine. Her face wears a complicated look full of gratitude and grief, inferiority and anger, all at the same time. Outside, twilight aches amethyst.

Sabiha boards the bus with Hira's *keffiyeh* hugging her shoulders. Someone's body odor isn't taking no for an answer. The plastic seat freezes the bejeezus beneath her skirt. She misses her jeans, abandoned in her locker. The bus passes Oscar Grant Plaza, which is empty. In her head, Sabiha hears the throaty unhappiness of an oboe.

The bus rolls to a stop miles before the intersection. A sea of brown, pin pricked by ovals of white, pools at the center of the traffic lights. It's a giant sleepover under a gray lid of clouds. The *Black Lives Matter* protestors have staged a die-in to plague the evening rush hour.

Sabiha watches her hand receive a signal from somewhere she does not know and press the "Stop Requested"

ALEX POPPE

button. Her body leads. Her feet keep time to a quick percussion like congas playing in a park until she is halfway down the block. Her brain follows. At the perimeter of the die-in, dead silence coats the reclining bodies. There's a sizzle in the air that Sabiha recognizes as possibility. She walks the dotted line map of feet meeting heads until space enough for her opens on the ground. As she lies down, she's sure she's on the verge of pleasure. This shimmering feeling is invisible and everywhere. The people on either side of her take her hands.

'Thanks for coming out.' The words are strung together like additions to an add-a-pearl necklace. After all, the protestors are supposed to be dead.

'Of course. No problem.' Sabiha wears a new face.

'It's cool having one of you support one of us. Peace.'

Sabiha feels her skin sprout steel scales. When she speaks, her voice has a caramel edge. 'Muslim lives matter too.' Her neighbor grasps her hand tighter. His fingers are warmly moist and slightly disgustingly cozy.

From nowhere, a necklace of floating diamonds encircles the die-in. A sea of sound rushes the protestors: rocks spanking concrete, glass shattering into teardrops, a stampede of cops moving in. The hands holding Sabiha's play a tug-of-war as they pull her up. Her eyes stream. The air tastes like bitter fire and it's getting hard to breathe.

'Wait! My backpack!' In her bag, the Rehana photo beats like a heart. Sabiha wishbones her right hand free to retrieve her bag and stumbles in the process. A lone shot cracks the air. Cocooning her bag, she's lifted up by a tide of people running. Sabiha runs too, and in her mind the dry Oakland asphalt sprouts lush green grass and slants uphill. She is running with Rehana, running with the Kurds, running

GIRL, WORLD

with the mountains into safety. The icy pitch of syncopated piano keys scores her retreat.

The protestors scatter like lab mice freed into a world they can't wait to explore. Sabiha smiles a private smile as she runs – she can't help smiling – this is the most alive she has ever felt. Now she understands why the Al-Zawra website instructs girls to train every day. Protest is hard work. She wonders if she should give up Kit-Kats.

Up ahead, a boy and girl, running and still holding hands, disappear into the seam of two buildings. Sabiha follows as much from lack of choice as from curiosity. There is an alley, nearly invisible from the street. Inside its trellised entrance, leaves glitter as they shiver. Sabiha doesn't feel the cold yet; sweat spiders her eyebrows. Somewhere a siren screeches.

'Hey.' A whisper stretches from a cartwheel of grass in the back left corner. It belongs to the girl whose eyes have a teaspoon of shadow under each of them.

'Hi. I followed you.' Sabiha's tongue hangs like a wilted flag.

'No problem. No one wants to get caught.' The boy has eyes of polished blue stone.

'Yeah. What happens if you do?'

'First protest?' The girl coos like Sabiha is a child. 'No, it's all good. Better to start some time than no time. This is our seventh. We met at Occupy Oakland.'

Sabiha thinks about the Sisterhood working alongside their husbands. 'That's really romantic.'

Blue Eyes focuses on some distant place where protest is a religion. 'The cops usually just arrest you and bring you down to central booking. Sooner or later you get to go home.'

The word pumpkins her. 'Shit,' Sabiha, The Protestor swears. 'I need to go.' She adds her sweat to the *keffiyeh*

ALEX POPPE

before stuffing it in the bottom of her bag. 'Can you point me towards 27th and Telegraph Avenue please?'

※

Sirood is waiting for her at the door. He stands too close, inhaling sharply. Sabiha pushes past him.

'What gives?' Sabiha sniffs herself. Underneath her girl smell is the scent of independence blossoming. She is a peony spreading its petals.

'Have you been smoking?'

'What? No!' Sabiha burps into Sirood's face. It is a throwback to when she was a kid and would lean in to tell a secret but burp instead. 'See?'

A faint smile flirts with the corners of Sirood's mouth. 'Okay, I believe you.'

That burp works every time.

'I was worried. Why so late?'

Sabiha parks her hand on Sirood's shoulder as she peels off her shoes. 'There was a die-in during rush hour. The buses couldn't get through.'

'I saw it on TV.'

'I finally got off and walked.' Which is only a half lie. Which is why Sabiha feels only half guilty.

Sirood gets lost in a moment, 'Sorry, you looked just like Mom for a second. Listen, next time stay on the bus. It's safer than the street. Someone might think you're a protestor. You could get arrested.'

Sabiha tunes out Sirood to hear the hum of things: the television murmuring in the living room and the buzz of light bulbs illuminating the hallway. She chews the insides of her cheeks to keep from saying *So?* and sends her softest

GIRL, WORLD

voice out from between her lips. 'You're right. Next time I'll be more careful.' Why did it take so long to realize how easy this is? People want to hear what they want to hear. This adult thing is so simple. Sabiha sees an older version of herself slung diagonally across an armchair.

Sirood goes into the kitchen. 'Mom went to the gym. I can heat some leftovers. How does that sound?'

Sabiha's so hungry that leftovers make her feel lucky. She answers over the kiss of the fridge. 'Yeah, sounds great.' She doesn't care if those leftovers were being made as Sirood talked to their father.

Later, in the shower, where her thoughts are always honest, Sabiha confronts the day's events. Turning the water hotter doesn't erase that horrible knowing feeling, even as her flesh scalds. She lets the water pour. It is a voice washing over her: big-throated and primal, alive like a heart.

❋

Lavender light filters through the library window, hazing the computer room. It's been five days and twenty-three hours since Sabiha found Shams' blog *Diary of a Caliphette* on Tumblr and five days and twenty-one hours since Shams friended Sabiha on Facebook.

ALEX POPPE

THUR 3:47 PM

OMG. Sabiha, have you tried those peanut butter Kit-Kats? Way better than white ☺

The white Twix is better than the Kat.

I'll have to try. Bring some if you come. You'll die over this new liner I got. My sister brought it back from Gaziantep. They have more choice than here. It's like five thousand times more silky. Ooooh She brought pistachios too ☺ I'm gonna get fat.

GIRL, WORLD

> LOL. Hardly. I'm sure working at the hospital keeps you skinny.

> I love what I'm doing now. There are too many broken kids, thanks to ASSad. This war is heartbreaking. I'm glad I made *hijra*.

> I could never.

> Sure you could if you want. That ask.fm website tells you how to get here and join jihad. It's easier than you think. Most things in life usually are. Just get to Turkey. From there, Syria is a snap.

ALEX POPPE

This girl is so cool! Sabiha flicks through Shams' photos on Facebook while they message back and forth. Envy bites her insides. Shams is *living*! Sabiha wishes they could Skype. She bets the music of Shams' voice is bold and triumphant, like Metallica covered by the San Francisco Symphony.

> Anyway, let's finish this quiz. Don't you want to know which of the Prophet's wives you're most like?

> I hope I'm an Aisha ☺

> I'm a Maryam ☺

> Everyone wants to be a Maryam. She bore the Prophet's son, she could sing, she was gorgeous. But Aisha had fire. She was a warrior. She did things.

GIRL, WORLD

> Ok, SabAisha. Number 6: What is your preferred hairstyle? A) Pinned loosely to your head; B) Cascading down your shoulders; C) However my husband prefers it.

> I like Rehana's braid.

> She's a Kurd. They fight against us. I'm glad one of our holy warriors beheaded her.

> Sabiha?

> Are you there?

ALEX POPPE

> Sabibti?

> ????????

> Cascading down my shoulders.

> Number 7: If you were an animal, what kind of animal would you be? A) Lion; B) Falcon; C) Kitten.

> Falcon

GIRL, WORLD

What is your weapon of choice?
A) AK-47; B) Knife; C) Suicide vest/explosives.

Ugh. None of the above.

Not a choice. You wouldn't say that if you saw what the world is doing to us over here. It's trying to make being alive unbearable. I'm going to send you some pics.

AK-47?

ALEX POPPE

> How can you best serve the new Islamic Utopia? A) Doctor; B) Soldier, C) Child Bearer.

> Soldier

> Right. You can't even pick a weapon. I'm marking Child Bearer. Okay, last one: Describe your ideal Prince Charming: A) Tall, dark and bearded; B) Short, dark and bearded; C) Whomever Allah sees fit.

> Really???!!!

GIRL, WORLD

What "Really"?

C

Of course C. Okay, you have a score of 17. You're a Zaynab, which is almost as good as an Aisha. She stood by Aisha when all of Medina turned against her. Loyalty rocks. Plus she made like totally beautiful handicrafts and sold them to benefit the household and gave money to the poor. You'll have no prob finding a husband.

Do you like being married?

ALEX POPPE

> Yeah! My life has meaning. I support my husband in building a new society where everyone matters. I'm part of it. Plus it's fun trying to make babies ☺

> I could never marry someone I didn't know.

> I could introduce you to a few warriors on FB. You could chat and get to know each other the right way. You learn the real person, the inside, instead of thinking you love someone because he looks like that judge on Arab Idol.

> Or Channing Tatum. I love him ♥

GIRL, WORLD

> Me too ♥ We could find you your very own right here.

> I dunno.

> Think about it. You really need to get a smart phone. Listen I have to get to the hospital. Sending a few pics now. Bye SabAisha.

> Thanks Shams. Bye ☺

A piano note heralds the arrival of photo attachments. The first one is a makeshift ward of melted, bloody children who were gassed by Assad. They died open-mouthed, like baby birds. Sabiha stares at the photo until her heart bangs against the bars.

ALEX POPPE

It's the kind of photo that doesn't let you shirk responsibility. And Shams lives it, works it, strives to stop it.

The next photo is a smiling fighter holding up a woman's severed head. A long blond braid trails past the floating orb like a kite tail. Janis Joplin screeches raw violet in Sabiha's inner ear. Her stomach swoops to her mouth as she chokes back a bit of puke. She puts her hands to her own neck, resting them on her butter knife collar bones until her stomach calms. She gets Rehana's "V" photo from her backpack and holds it to the computer screen. "V" Rehana has open eyes, a butterscotch face, and a neck propping up her head. Dead Rehana has closed eyes, a white face, and bloody lacey edges where a neck should be. The smiling fighter has a body, neck, and head, topped with a backwards baseball cap. The smiling fighter and "V" Rehana wage a staring contest. Sabiha opens Google and "V" Rehana wins.

According to *MailOnLine*, Rehana, alive and well, escaped to southern Turkey. Sabiha sees her running under a blueberry sherbet sky, running over soil that is less like cookie dough and more like cookie crumbs as she crosses the border, her defiant, streaming braid the color of a lemon wheel when you hold it to the sun. Full of gratitude, Sabiha's heart beats a chocolaty dum-tee-dum.

How could Shams have gotten it so wrong? Sabiha's heart hardens to a peach pit. A pinwheel in her mind rotates the faces of everyone who confuses her: Shams, Sirood, Jesse and his nipple-grazed girlfriend, her father. In that moment she hates them all, which really means she hates herself. She wishes she were in the pink cocoon of her bedroom, so she could fling herself onto her bubble gum bed and bite her pillow. In her mind's eye, Sabiha breathes in colors, soft rose and thistle, until the self-loathing she cannot name subsides

GIRL, WORLD

and her eyelashes no longer gleam. She shuts down the computer. Her reflection in the computer screen taunts her, like it wants to get her into trouble. Sabiha diverts her gaze through the window, to the stained-glass sky.

    Outside cool air kisses her face. Sabiha hears the wedding dress elegance of harp music as she approaches the bus stop. Across the street, a busker, all elbows and sharp angles, cradles the wooden frame, plucking at its strings. The delicate notes whirl across the street and pull Sabiha towards them. She laces through the crowd until she's close enough to feel the vibrations electrify each follicle of arm hair. When the harpist finishes playing, Sabiha roots inside her jacket pocket for some change. She has lost her taste for Kit Kats.

    'Thanks.' The harpist's voice is as milky as her skin.

    Sabiha wants to pluck the strings, to create the petalsoft music of dawn breaking with her own fingertips. She feels like a butterfly has landed on her index finger. She waits expectantly. The harpist resumes playing, not sparing another glance in Sabiha's direction. The size of the crowd ebbs and flows. As darkness cleaves to the streetlights, Sabiha jams her hands into her empty pockets and ambles towards the bus stop in her own private silence, slowly home.

Room 308

Sunlight streaked through the orange-red leaves, illuminating the dust motes hiding in the pale air. Bridget, the student nursing aide supervisor, was helping a chubby toddler feed the ducks in the artificial lake at the center of the grounds. Her gentle cooing skimmed over grass blades and floated up to the window, where I stood. My forehead was slick with a layer of oil. My scrub top was crusty with dried oatmeal, and my pockets were bloated with wadded Kleenex. Visitors' Day was winding down. On Visitors' Day, we got a lot of extended family and clergy and shiny people who came because the other people who came were shiny and felt guilty, and no one was too ashamed to cry big tears, and stay for a few hours to feel good about themselves and the time they had just put in, and they needed extra Kleenex from the student nursing aides who were always there.

I was watching Bridget skip across the soft lawn to deliver the child back to his mother. Like me, the mom stood apart, watching Bridget and her son. Beyond clarifying the intricacies of patient sponge baths, I never spoke to Bridget. We were separated by experience and by the fact that she pitied me. Bridget was twenty-four, which was four years more than my age, and we had spent every weekday of the autumn here. I did it because I was addicted to Xanax and Bridget did it because her brother was still deployed, and she believed that her helping someone over here would increase

GIRL, WORLD

the chances of someone helping him over there. Bridget swung the toddler high before placing him at his mother's empty side and nodded towards the window as she walked back to the main building of the VA hospital. The mother bent down to retie her son's sneaker laces and her skirt rode up, revealing a dancer's legs. I left the freshly cut grass smell of the open window and entered the Clorox air of the linen closet to check my stash, pausing to grab an alibi of bleached sheets. Bridget, trailing sunshine, passed me as I exited and crooked her finger for me to follow. Over her shoulder she told me there was a Teaching Point, a new patient, still unconscious from surgery, and we needed to monitor his vitals as he had just lost both his legs from the hip down. I didn't ask what'd happened to his in-between. She entered room 308 and led me into the stale dark. A fraction of a man lay in the bed. An endotracheal tube snaked past a faint harelip scar above his upper lip into his mouth, and even though his eyes were closed, I saw that this head and torso belonged to my ex-commanding officer. I stepped into the bedside table and knocked over a silver framed photograph of a beautiful mini-skirted woman with ballet legs holding a baby upright against her chest for the camera.

I'm sorry, I said. I was sorry I had said sorry.

Bridget's face wrinkled through a chain of causality. If A leads to B, and B leads to C; A results in C after which she said nothing, as if to say, Can you handle this? with an element of, You'd better handle this because he and others like him have sacrificed so much, so that you and I can stand here with our whole selves fully intact, so I said, It's okay, to mean I'm okay, I can handle this and so much more, so please continue to instruct me.

The next day was the start of Marine Fest, a three-day

ALEX POPPE

bacchanal during which thousands of marines would arrive and celebrate being marines in our very stately and very gracious town. On the last night of the festival, when the marines were decked out in their best Blue Dress "A"s, sipping cocktails in the Potomac Ballroom Library to celebrate the 239 birthday of the Marine Corps, I would be cleaning bed pans of loose stool because during that day and the one before, able-bodied marines would have visited their disabled half-bodied brethren and snuck them tastes of all they had been denied. During my rounds, the visiting marines would tell me to take extra good care of their boys, and they would laugh fatly to say, You are here to service, or they would wrap their fingers around my wrist to say, I could break you; except for those marines who exhaled briskly through their teeth as soon as they stepped back into the hallway. Those marines would slip me a fifty and say thank you with their eyes glued to their shoes and I would wonder at their imprudence and give the fifty to Dr. Bob, a fourth-year resident with a gambling problem and a liberated prescription pad. Dr. Bob lived in a high rise near the marina and claimed to know what every nursing aide tasted like.

Bridget knew about Dr. Bob but couldn't do much. She was small and Christian and dyed her hair blond and kept two extra pairs of ironed scrubs in her work locker so she could change if a guest had an unfortunate accident. She called the patients "guests" because she felt it added an element of optimism to the VA. The VA was very clean and very cold. Bridget led seminars on Turning and Positioning, and kept an eye on us. Most nights after her shift ended, she headed to the hospital chapel to log in a half-hour of prayer for the worst-offs. I overheard her tell an unconscious "guest" she did it to stock up brownie points with the Man Upstairs, and

GIRL, WORLD

would be happy to put a word in for the mummified man in the bed before her. She couldn't control the nursing aides in their free time, but she could make them clean bed pans on her time. All of the nursing aides did yoga and were blond and had Botox. Once a month, they pitched in and bought some black market syringes of filler and bribed a cosmetology technician to smooth their foreheads or plump out their lips and hands. Afterwards they'd hit Chihuahua's to sip frozen margaritas through extra-wide straws.

Dr. Bob rolled five marijuana cigarettes for a twenty in the dry-goods storage room behind the cafeteria in the basement, which is where Bridget would find us on the night of the Marine Corps Birthday Ball, and she would be in an uncharitable mood that evening because some of the marines who celebrated the Corps' birthday every year, a group of dog trainers for the Corps and not actual combat soldiers, husky, and raucous and braggadocio drunk, had cornered her by the hospital gift shop and sung her the Marines' Hymn with altered lyrics and Bridget had to smile like a girl unwrapping an expensive present she knew she was getting and shuffle over in her regulation shoes and thin cotton scrubs to shake each enormous calloused palm and gush You are our heroes! You are our heroes! and let the handshakes turn into full body hugs while each marine took his turn feeling her up. When Bridget found Dr. Bob and me lying across plastic-wrapped cartons of adult diapers smoking a joint, she would have some things to say about my blackened soul and some more things to say about my degenerate character, which was worse than a gutter-tramp's, and only one thing to say about the prospects of my future training as one of Her Certified Nursing Assistants.

ALEX POPPE

But this shift was winding down. I'd spent the last bit of it sitting with the patients who hadn't had any visitors, watching reruns of *The Price is Right* and betting on the over or under. Lance Corporal William Philips won a new car and my Caribbean cruise vacation in the Showcase Showdown, which made him happy because an ambush in the Anbar Province had taken his sight, so he didn't drive anymore. I fluffed his pillows during the commercial break and folded his fingers around a chocolate truffle because I remembered when I was a kid how excited I was when someone paid me a bit of special attention just because. The truffle was wrapped in fancy foil with a famous quote printed on the inside. When we were little, my sister had a desktop calendar with a fresh aphorism printed on each page of the year. Lying shoulder to shoulder on our stomachs with our bare feet dangling off the edge of her twin bed, we'd look for meaning in the convoluted words. We'd look for significance in anything, we wishers upon eyelashes.

The truffles came from a store-within-a-store inside the hospital gift shop. They were sold by Sonny who'd spent four years in a federal penitentiary for drug smuggling, following seven years on the lam. A DEA officer spotted him in the background of a Bud Light commercial, which is how he got caught; and then a local church organization led by a former New Orleans Saints' cheerleader thirty years past her prime organized a petition drive, which is how he got out early, two years ago at age seventy. Sonny often asked me how I could eat so much chocolate and still be as skinny as dripping water. He'd ask, Where do you put it? In my pocket, I'd say, and this much was true, so I didn't say anything else. He'd tsk his tongue against the roof of his mouth, but put a few extra pieces in my

GIRL, WORLD

bag. People who knew about Sonny's past compared him to Gene Hackman, and I think he liked that.

❋

I righted the silver-framed photo which still had its worn price tag stuck on the back. My ex-commanding officer was my ex-adjudicator and had signed off on my discharge without benefits. He was once a strong and beautiful man. His wife, probably his wife, entered as I was recording his pulse and respiration rate. I say probably his wife because, although he wore no ring and had never had at the School of Infantry, Camp Geiger, she did. The two-carat solitaire caught the last rays of sunlight streaming around the edges of the blinds covering the window. I figured this ring to be a neon announcement of worth, a quantification of how much she was loved, to the world, and I felt sorry for her, and for myself, to be caring for my ex-commanding officer here, in this place of broken people, and for her to see that her handsome husband was now a half-man, and no amount of prayer or medical miracles or stored up good deeds was going to restore the other half. She was in a lose-lose situation because if she stayed with him, she would grow to hate him and if she left him, she would hate herself, at least for a little while, and if she stayed and had an affair, then all his comrades-in-arms would hate her, unless the affair was with a fellow marine that her husband had pre-approved. In the right now, she'd need a robust mental Bluray collection because he would never again be with her in that way a man is with a woman, similar to but not the same as the way he was with me, which was why I was no longer part of the Marine Corps. I was an excellent misjudge of character; this ability was, in part, why

ALEX POPPE

a year ago I was nursing broken ribs and a bruised back at the Camp Geiger infirmary.

I was standing with the patient clipboard against my chest. The wife slid into the spouse-spot on the window side of the bed. Bridget was watching to make sure I didn't upset her or anything else in the room, and I thought about excusing myself so I would not have to watch the wife's fragile shoulders move up and down like creased wings, but marines are taught to suck it up and move forward, and if I left now, Bridget would think I was delicate, and she had little regard for me as it was.

Bridget offered to check on the wife's toddler, who was probably being fed chocolate fudge brownies from the Get Well Soon! baskets that piled up in the nurses station, to give her some moments alone with her husband. Because Bridget regarded me as an extension of herself when she was teaching, I returned the clipboard to its naked tack and prepared to leave. But the wife blinked with incomprehension so I doubted she equated the still bundle in bed with her understanding of husband. She introduced herself as Ashley and said that we should stay, she didn't wish to inconvenience us, and we should go about our business as if she weren't there. Then she told us what good people we were to be doing what we were doing, and because I don't like to talk, Bridget said thank you and regifted her praise to all the men and women in uniform who serve this great nation and to God, who always got praised by Bridget in case he was listening. I don't think Ashley was on speaking terms with God because that's when she interrupted Bridget with a snorting cough and turned her eyes on me, looking at me for a long moment. Bridget followed Ashley's stare to the dried oatmeal dotting my shirt and suggested I excuse myself to change my scrub top.

GIRL, WORLD

I nodded at Bridget's advice and exited. I didn't want to feel sympathy for Ashley. I didn't want to fold her jeweled fingers around truffles wrapped in inspirational foil because she had been loved and cherished by my ex-commanding officer and he had broken me. I walked past the nurses station where their son was sitting on a desktop boxing with a Tweety Bird balloon tied to a gift basket handle. He cried Duck! every time he hit the bird's face, and it arced low to the floor before coming back for more, and the little boy would laugh a sound like splashing water.

Bridget probably knew I didn't keep an extra scrub top in my locker. No abandoned shirts lay on the changing room floor. I rubbed at the dried oatmeal with some wet paper towels, which shed a layer of soapy paper dandruff along the institutional green-colored cloth. Standing in my bra to wash my shirt in the sink, I imagined how Bridget and Ashley's patient-care conversation would go:

New trainee?
Yes.
Any good?
No.
Think she'll improve?
Probably not, bless. But God never gives us more than we can bear.

❊

I visited Lefty, an artillery gunner who liked when I read to him. We were working our way through *Something Wicked This Way Comes* when Bridget stopped by his open door and beckoned me. Bookmarking our place with a truffle, I laid the paperback beside his pillow and told Lefty I would

ALEX POPPE

see him later. When I stood, Bridget pursed her lips at the wet patches on my uniform top.

I thought I told you to always have an extra uniform at work.

I forgot.

Do you know the new patient?

I bent down to pick up some invisible lint so I would need to wash my hands. My scrub pants were too long, and where the hem dragged on the ground was outlined in gray. I straightened and crossed to the sink. Over the sound of running water, Bridget recycled her question.

Do you know him?

No.

Bridget checked Lefty's chart and exited. I followed about half a pace behind.

I'll need to pray for him tonight.

Yeah.

After you do a bed pan check on the floor, you can go.

Okay. Great.

Are you going out tonight?

I don't know.

You've still got slop on your shirt. Since you're not going out, you'll have plenty of time to launder and press *two* fresh shirts for your next shift. I want to *see* them before you go on the floor. Am I understood?

Yes, I said. I wondered if Bridget was going out after her all-inclusive chapel stop and if she had any friends either. Even though she meant well, in her own way, the other nursing aides kept their distance. Bridget was pretty in that conventional style that women found reassuring and men found non-threatening, so she'd probably never had a locked and loaded .45 held at the base of her skull as someone older and

GIRL, WORLD

of a higher rank than she pulled down her pants against her will and made her cry. I could imagine Bridget marrying one of the charity cases in wheelchairs, an officer candidate friend of her brother's, someone with a short life expectancy and a generous pension payout, someone who told blond jokes and could not fuck his wife but actually liked women.

I went into the supply closet where I kept my stash. With the door shut, it was colorless and quiet inside, and I liked it because then I was just a person in a supply closet in a hospital. My fingertips grazed the stacks of starched, clean sheets, some of which were rough and some of which smelled like a Chinese dry cleaner's. From my stockpile of Xanax, I slid an orally disintegrating tablet under my tongue and waited for my blood to stop crackling and for my conscious mind to settle into that zone between drunkenness and consequence. I took only half the dosage, in case I ran into Bridget again, and stored the other half inside my bra cup.

❋

To the bed pans. In Staff Sergeant Mohammad Aksari's room, a lively poker game was in full swing when I came in. Staff Sergeant Mohammad Aksari was a career officer with seven tours of duty split between Iraq and Afghanistan under his belt. Many of the marines who cycled in and out of the VA had served with or under him, and he was popular because of his knowledge of Arabic and his commitment to the Corps. He sat in bed with his knobby potato toes sticking out from under the blanket. Sometimes when I gave him a sponge bath, he'd tell to do my duty and suck him off. I'd say, *Habir*, which I thought meant "dick" in Arabic but which I later learned meant "expert". The poker game cloaked me in invisibility

ALEX POPPE

so I left his bed pan where it lay before marking zero output on his chart and slipping away.

Dusk had shifted to stars. From room 308's doorway, I saw that Ashley had gone, maybe to take her son home or to get something to eat, so I entered. The room felt womblike. In its soft opacity my ex-commanding officer looked as dignified as he had on that first day of School of Infantry training. In the corridor, footsteps were ushering the full-bodied outside, back among the living. The headlights on their cars were guiding the drivers away from the VA hospital, probably towards the marina. At midnight, there would be amateur fireworks you could watch from the promenade. This was in anticipation of the Corps' birthday. It was part of the town's effort to make the visiting servicemen and women feel appreciated in a world grown weary of war. Since my discharge, I had been living in a nearby beach town, renting a room from a medicated bipolar heiress who dabbled in interior design and was a devotee of face yoga. When her parents divorced early the next year, and her father's new girlfriends began refurnishing his many residences, she would find herself out of a decorating job and move to Los Feliz to try to break into stunt work. She'd try for movies, and then for television, and then for commercials, and finally for computer games. I'm still waiting to see her Claymation head being decapitated from her anatomically-enhanced body when I play *Assassin's Creed* on my PlayStation. I would like for something big to happen for her because she never said a word when I sampled from her bathroom's well-stocked medicine cabinet, and particularly because on the evening of the Corps Birthday Ball, when Bridget discovered my prone body across boxes of adult incontinence products, a Dr. Bob at my side and his

GIRL, WORLD

joint in my hand, and after clearing out my locker and being escorted off the premises, I would arrive home to an empty apartment with full pill bottles which I'd empty, and because the emergency medical technicians would smell marijuana on me, they'd call the police who'd search the house and find my roommate's hidden cache which I hadn't known she had, which would make this the last autumn she lived in this beach town.

    I settled into a chair in the corner of the room and marveled at where my ex-commanding officer's legs used to be. He had practiced martial arts and used to deliver a mean roundhouse kick. This man, my former commanding officer for whom I would have risked my life once upon a time ago, was so still, so motionless that I felt a certain grief. Because he was no longer the Man In Charge, he no longer owned the truth.

    We'd met on the first day of School of Infantry classroom instruction. He epitomized the ideal marine: courageous, honorable, committed. He told me what to expect during the twenty-nine day Marine Combat Training Course and promised to impart the knowledge and ability necessary to operate in a combat environment. He made me feel at home and said he'd show me the ropes to get me qualified. Later, he spoke to me privately about not wearing makeup around the other recruits or running in jogging shorts because some marines viewed the women on the base as walking mattresses who were there only to be fucked, and I would be asking for it if I did either of those things because who doesn't capitalize on an opportunity that's presented to him, and I didn't want to be charged with conduct unbecoming did I, and to remember that boys and girls and alcohol just don't mix and from that point on only he would be able to sign off on my qualifications and I should come to his

ALEX POPPE

barracks for those signatures. I might have sneered a little, I don't know because I can't control it, and in times of great tension or danger I sneer. That's when he started sleeping in my bed. I'd come in from training to find him sprawled across my mattress, and then I'd have to wait inside my car, which was the only place he didn't have a key, until he woke up and went away. When I finally reported him to the higher-ups, I was asked if I had a boyfriend and was told that I was weak to complain about him just because I didn't like him. One of them suggested I was a hot little mess who was trying to destroy the Corps, and maybe I should be tested for a personality disorder.

The door to the room opened. I should have jumped up and pretended that I was doing something other than sitting in the semi-darkness with a rehearsal corpse, but that Xanax had kicked in so I didn't. It was Miss Patty the Tex-Mex floor nurse who was on husband number five and therefore impossible to surprise. It's bath time, was all she said, and then, Give me a hand. I filled a small bowl with warm, soapy water and gathered some supplies. Miss Patty leaned over the bed and pulled my ex-commanding officer towards her. Get the tie, she said.

I didn't want to get the tie because then I might touch him, and I didn't want to see a spread of flesh that was both strong and weak at the same time, and I didn't want to be close enough to smell his dead-weather smell, but I got the tie because that is what student nursing aides do, and more important, that is what marines do, and it wasn't as bad as bringing him his coffee after he kicked my legs out from underneath me when I had gone to his office to retrieve the supply closet keys so I could feed the station dogs as part of my nightly cleanup duty at Camp Geiger. Miss Patty gently

GIRL, WORLD

laid my ex-commanding officer back against his pillows, then drew the gown up past his shoulders and chest. There wasn't much left of the area below his belly button. The part that wasn't covered in plaster and bandages looked like it had been through a shark attack. Tiny beads of perspiration formed above my upper lip and I used my lower lip to wipe them away. Ok, Miss Patty said, but she was looking at me, then Ok Handsome, and she was looking at him, We're going to give you a little spa treatment so you can rest more comfortably during the night, even though he wasn't conscious to hear her, and then she sponged at his face, neck, chest, and arms as one would a newborn. I took away the damp used cloths and gave Miss Patty clean ones before I rolled my ex-commanding officer onto his side so Miss Patty could clean his back. I was surprised he seemed as heavy now as he had then, when he had used his body to pin me down on the barracks' floor, because there was so little left of him. Is there anything else you need me to do? I asked and when Miss Patty shook her head I exited into the mall-lit hallway.

Ashley had just stepped off the elevator and was walking towards my ex-commanding officer's room. Oh, you're still here, she said but she didn't sound surprised, to which I said, Yes, and then we stared at each other like two people who don't know each other and therefore have nothing to say. The whites of her eyes were hacked by tiny broken blood vessels. Well, I said and took a step around her, which she countered with, Wait, and then, I am so sad, which was said so quietly that I wasn't sure if it had come from her or me. I took a truffle from my pocket and held it out to her. This might help, I said. When she didn't respond, I explained, There's an inspirational message on the inside. Ashley didn't take the candy so I added, It tastes good too, and then lifted

ALEX POPPE

her left hand from where it hung at the side of her body and formed her fingers into a tiny cup. It might help with the sadness, I said as I dropped the chocolate into her palm and closed her fingers around it. I turned and walked away because I had just lied to her. Nothing eased the sadness.

Thank you, she said as she caught up to me. You must be tired after such a long day. Would you like to have some coffee? I told her I didn't drink coffee and needed to get going, which was another lie because there was no one and nothing waiting for me anywhere. She opened her mouth to say something but her words got caught in her throat, which made her face look like a fish's. I smiled at this, and she must have taken my smile as reconsideration because she closed her mouth and swallowed and looked at me the way a pretty child looks at the new kid before she invites her to play. Then she said she would like, if it wasn't too much trouble, for me to sit with her in the hospital cafeteria while she worked up the nerve to enter her husband's room. She said she had asked me because she could see that I was a kind person, a good person, a person her husband would like, and my giving her the truffle had confirmed this. I kept my face very still, and tried not to think, as I followed her into the elevator and we stood side by side silently watching the floor numbers light up in descending succession, about what her husband might say if he knew his wife had decided to confide in me, or if he'd worry that I might share a few secrets too, or if any of what he'd done to me had affected his life at all.

I sat at an out-of-the-way table as Ashley stood in line. At this late hour the cafeteria was almost empty, and most of the kitchen staff were smoking cigarettes in the alley beside the delivery dock as they played Frisbee with their hair nets.

GIRL, WORLD

The place stank of tater tots. The chime of china shattering against ceramic tiles pierced the chicken-fried air. A litany of Spanish swear words rang out from the dishwasher. Across the fluorescent bulb dining room, Miss Patty momentarily lifted her head from the romance novel she was reading, and then sipped discreetly from a black chrome flask she kept tucked away within her ample bosom. She flexed and pointed her toes, which were propped up on the chair across from her. My stomach growled. I unwrapped a chocolate. *An eye for an eye leaves the world blind*, is what the wrapper read, which was said by Gandhi, which figured. I crumpled it into a ball and shot it across the table at the bottoms of Miss Patty's feet as Ashley returned with a coffee and a bottle of water. In case you change your mind, she said as she placed the water in front of me and slid into the adjacent seat. Thanks, I said but I didn't mean it.

I don't know why but I'm afraid to see him, she blurted.

Because you don't want to face what your life has become, but I didn't say that. Instead I said that it had to be hard.

You must see patients like him all the time. Does it get to you?

No, I said and for the first time I told her something true.

How not?

I lay the bottle of water on its side and spun it on the table.

Why do you work here? Do you have family in the military?

My father was a Chief Petty Officer and my grandfather retired as a Sergeant Major. Where was your husband deployed? I didn't tell her that the last time I had seen him was at Camp Geiger.

He went to Afghanistan seven months ago, she said, twisting her diamond ring along her delicate finger, as if

ALEX POPPE

to say, You made me a promise, but not very forcefully so as to say, You betrayed me; obviously you can't be trusted; obviously you failed me and your country.

 C'mon, I said as I stood, Let's go. It won't get any easier.

✽

We stopped shoulder to shoulder outside room 308. Do you want to go in alone? I asked to show her she couldn't back down.

 No, she said, Could we enter together?

 Ok, I said as I opened the door and gave her a little hard shove forward. I hung back as she approached my ex-commanding officer. His body added contour to the upper two-thirds of the bed while the lower third of the bed was flat.

 Ashley stood in the spouse-spot shaking her head.

 What, I asked, but I did not go to her.

 He doesn't look like himself, she said.

 I wanted to laugh a little, but I didn't.

 It's the facial hair. He would never let himself go like that.

 This much was true. I had never seen him look less than recruitment poster ready, not even when he grabbed his loaded .45 and chambered the round inches from my ear.

 Do you think we could shave him?

 I imagined holding a sharp blade next to his jugular.

 Do you think you could show me how? Are you trained to do that? The wife asked.

 I'm trained to do that, I said. I raised the head of the bed so my ex-commanding officer was in a seated position. Imagine if he had awoken right then. Imagine his surprise. I could not look directly at his face, but I thought about holding the skin under his jaw firmly and tightly as I ran a razor along it. I need

GIRL, WORLD

to get some supplies, I said as I turned toward the doorway. I exited.

I walked down the hall past the supply closet to the stairs.

Once inside the stairwell, I sat down on a step and pressed my sticky forehead to the metal railing. Then I extracted the other half of the Xanax from my bra and placed it under my tongue. I waited for a while, during which I am sure, Ashley found another nurse's aide to gather shaving cream and towels and a razor, and show her how to shave her half-husband.

I took the stairs to the garage park and headed for my car. As I was fumbling for my keys among truffle wrappers and used Kleenexes, I heard a familiar God praising voice. I ducked down between my car and the next, just as Dr. Bob strolled by, ruffling Bridget's hair and then cupping her behind.

You did good today, he said.

MOXIE

Bet you'd like one huh? Sucks to be you. I'll eat the whole fucking bag if I want to. Today is I-don't-give-a-fuck-day so stop looking at me. Sit somewhere else. You're blocking my view.

One point one million people ride the New York City subway every day, and it feels like half of them are here right now in this car on the Brooklyn-bound L. Hipsters packed in so tight their beards are meshing. NPR says if you have a beard, you have a better chance of getting a job in IT. That's real good news for women.

How long before that guy rocking the Supreme tee and sag-ass skater bottoms cups that Puerto Rican-Asian girl's *culo*? She's a melting pot jackpot. Those PR curves with that Asian skin. I believe her advertising. Look at them talking, teeth chattering in love. I think it will happen as we go through the East River Tunnel. I'll bet you the rest of these Reese's Peanut Butter Cups. Unless you're one of those artisanal craft chocolate fucks on your way to Mast Brothers. What have you got for me?

Damn he's slick. We're not even at First Avenue. I give them six weeks, tops. Then he'll realize she sounds like a wife-magazine article or she'll experience his pettiness. Everything fresh has a shelf life.

Jesus that bitch there is loud. No one pushed her and now she's acting like, just because she lost the genetic lottery, the

GIRL, WORLD

world is conspiring to make her shitty little life just a bit more miserable. We should stick everyone who is fucked off with the world into a huge wave pool until they remember how to like themselves again. I'd be the first one in.

It's hot. That guy with the origami belly is panting like he's going to expire any minute. Would you offer assistance? One of my exes is a paramedic. He's like an Abercrombie and Fitch model with a little Michael Pitt thrown in for some downtown edge. Can you imagine some rom-com set up where you've been kicked curbside like some recycled fuck-toy, and you wake up to his ruby reds blowing the breath of life back into you? Eyes click in mutual recognition, and there's this moment of heart courage, and you dare to believe in a better version of yourself. Then six weeks later, see above.

The better version of myself is lounging rooftop poolside at King & Grove Lifestyle Hotel drinking Perrier Jouet with the tooth fairy. Kissing distance to the sky, I am kind, I am beautiful, I am whole. My right cheek is not the texture of crunchy peanut butter, nor is it singed dark like chocolate coating. I do not snap the rubber band on my wrist until pain-darts pierce my skin, shrapnel tearing. I am half-dark, half-light; two-faced when turned-cheek. A yes-no face. If a bullet is a mouthful of pennies, how much is shrapnel?

The train sighs as it slinks into the belly of the Bedford Avenue station. The doors open and close like heart ventricles pumping damp air into the car. A rat races down the subway steps reaching the platform just as the doors close. The train resets its forward motion. Arms and legs enwombing her cello, a busker on the platform adds a touch of grace to the cacophony of man and machine. A pig-tailed toddler in her father's lanky arms points in my direction and cries. Ditching the bag of Reese's in the trash, I surface at street level behind

ALEX POPPE

Supreme tee and PR-Asian hybrid. Together they walk, a tangle of curves and limbs, toward the residential section of Greenpoint. Their cut-out forms shrinky-dink into the lazy chaos of storefront pubs and crowded taco trucks. Sweat slides into the bowl of my back.

Is it cheating or using or just the shit that happens when you yell out someone else's name during sex? What if your partner has had half her face singed and shredded? Can you ask her to wear a bag over her head or to turn her head so only her good side shows? Do you do her from behind or do you leave her behind? Can you lose life-luggage?

Snap, snap, snap goes the rubber band against my wrist. Snap, snap, snap turns my wrist hot numb. Snap, snap, snap hatchets red lines across blue veins. Breathe. This stretch of Bedford Avenue has more missing person fliers than it used to. We are a generation of lost people. What happens to their Facebook pages? I never recognize anyone from these posters but that doesn't stop me from looking into the eyes on the building sides. Permission to stare granted. I will probably never have gentle sex again.

The abandoned girdle factory on Bedford has been converted into a Premiere Retail Destination so trust fund babies feel ethically consumptive as they pay way too much for pre-torn shirts. Next door is an animal shelter housing other orphans of the city. I have already decided on a dog. It's that one. The one with the black eye in the white face. My muzzle nuzzles her neck. She smells like snow. Blotting my eyes on her fur, I feel her heartbeat pulse against my nose. It is tiny. She is fragile. We are scared. Holding her eye to my eye, her nose to my nose, she licks at my mouth. Head on, she does not turn away. Moxie.

After leashing Moxie, we head toward the skeletal

GIRL, WORLD

buildings that line the waterfront. Moxie sticks her butt up and waves it like the Queen's hand as she walks. There used to be raves here before some developer realized this section of Brooklyn was worth something and pushed the Poles north, the Puerto Ricans east, and the hookers out. A Vietnam vet with graying dreads photographed tourists in Rock Center by day and squatted here by night. He once gave me a white rose sandwiched between two red ones – said it reminded him of my smile – while we were waiting on the subway platform. Then he asked me for dinner. Moxie's ears prick at the bleating of a foghorn from somewhere along the East River. I don't do dinner.

Back in my apartment, Moxie pees the hardwood on entry. Her tail thumps the floor like she owns the place. Fuck nuts! I'm out of paper towel. There's not even The *New York Times* to wipe it up. I don't relish the thought of piss-soaked toilet tissue lodged under my fingernails. Stashing her in the bath, I start rummaging – which is how I find them lazing under some old tear sheets. That Absolut Ritts ad. That ad was... The rubber band bites my wrist. The rubber band breaks. If a bullet is a mouthful of pennies, how much is shrapnel? Fucking useless writing it all down, saving it all up. Where do memories go when you die? Finally these old journal pages are good for something. Hello yellow puddle.

Tomorrow. Is. Really. Happening!!! I get on my first plane. The test shots were great. I don't have to go to school for TWO WEEKS because of this shoot. There is talk of maybe the summer in PARIS. I hope Mom lets me go. I so can't wait for life to start. I hate school. Creepy Mr. Motts is always writing little notes on my labs reports. In biology, all the boys were snickering every time Mr. Motts said penis because it sounded like benis. He can't say his p's!!! Then

ALEX POPPE

Ryan Huff asked if the only time the stuff came out was to make a baby. Everyone knows that he and Kaley Kec are already doing it. He just wanted to mess with Mr. Motts but it back-splashed on me because Mr. Motts coughed a lot and said no. Sometimes it comes out when you are alone. He was looking at ME when he said it. I think other people saw because I heard snickering, and then my cheeks went all hot. Shit, I hear Mom crying. Steve Jacek asked Samantha Jacobs to sit on his face when Mr. Motts was explaining a diagram of lady parts, and then he called Samantha Jacobs Six-Pack-Sam and all the basketball players laughed. What's so funny about beer? I didn't get it but I pretended to.

The photographer at the test shoot (his name is Jeff☺) wanted to know if I was at least sixteen. I sort of lied and said yes. It's only a lie for the next twenty-three days. He looked down and smiled at his camera when I answered. Then he told me to look at him, not the camera, and then he moved closer and closer shooting film the whole time until we were like six inches apart, just looking at each other. Everything went still. It was like permission to stare, to really look at each other. And then he took the tips of his fingers and brushed them against my left cheek and told me I was so beautiful. I swear I didn't breathe once the whole time. My cheek still feels tingly where he touched it. Mom tells me I'm beautiful all the time but this was different. This time I believed it.

'Moxie,' I call, freeing her from the bathtub. She likes being scratched behind the ears. 'Let's go.' It's Miller time.

✣

'Kaifa.' I greet Alat, the bartender. He was a child soldier in Somalia and looks at all my face when he talks to me. Most

GIRL, WORLD

people pick a side: stare at the right in disgusted sympathy or stare at the left in concentrated politeness.

'Marhaba habibi. Hamdullah. Kaifik,' which is his standard reply of welcome dear, I am good, praise Allah. How are you?

'Hamdullah.' Alat knows that's as far as my Arabic goes: handler greetings. 'Do you mind if I bring my dog in?' Moxie is already inside, running the leash around my ankles, but I am not a total twat when it comes to niceties. She rocks her butt from side to side at Alat. How could he resist? Good dog.

'Is it trained?'

'Yes!' I say as I shake my head no. 'But she just peed on my floor so I think we're good for a while.'

'Better take it into the beer garden.'

'Is there air conditioning?' I deadpan. Being spoiled dies hard.

Alat gives me *a look*. 'What's its name?'

'Moxie.' I untangle my feet from her leash to introduce them. 'Alat, Moxie. Moxie, Alat.'

Moxie licks and licks the three leftover fingers on Alat's right hand. He doesn't talk about how he lost the other two and I don't talk about how I lost half my face. It's our unspoken pact. Shit, I need to feed her. It's been a while since I've had to think about anyone except myself.

'The usual?'

'And chase it with a beer. It's still hot outside.'

The beer garden is half-crowded. A few heads turn.

Is that...? No, it couldn't be. Jesus! What happened to her? Imagining the questions is like going to your own funeral. When people can't believe their eyes, they are looser with their tongues.

Shit. I know that girl in the corner rocking the baby

carriage. She was an up and comer like me until a bad coke habit flushed her down. Her nostrils look red and chapped from where I'm sitting. Good luck kid.

Alat arrives with my drinks and a bowl of water for Moxie. 'Thanks.' She gulps it down and starts licking my toes. 'You don't happen to have any food she can eat.' I turn my head so only my good side shows and give Alat my cover girl smile.

That's what he sees. From the sidewalk opposite the beer garden. And that's what draws Abercrombie-and-Fitch-with-a-bit-of-Michael-Pitt to the beer garden's perimeter. The smile of my former self. I can almost hear his tumbleweed whispered 'Jax?' as he approaches. My palms itch.

'Jax. I can't believe it. It is you. Stay right there. I'm coming in.' At the sound of my name, Coke Nose gasps in my direction. I subtly thumb my nostrils in return.

'Alat, another please,' and shoot back my Black Label.

This is stupid. I can't sit in profile the whole night. I usually hiss at people when they point at my face. He's not going to point. I have about ten seconds to decide on a strategy. No seconds. Here he is holding a beer.

He's so beautiful it hurts to look at him. His lips are the color of red gummy bears and cushiony. His skin is so smooth you want to trace it with your fingertips. Looking up at him, I feel less than who I am. Shake it off girl. Turning my head, I look straight at him and cock my right eyebrow.

He doesn't outwardly flinch. As a paramedic, he's probably used to seeing gruesome sights. My heart beats in my ears. Moxie breaks the silence with a few soft barks. 'Who's that?' He sits down and reaches for her under the table.

'Moxie.' Moxie licks his fingers savagely. She's got good taste.

GIRL, WORLD

'I think she's hungry.' He wipes his hand on his jeans. Moxie resumes licking my toes.

'Yeah,' I feel like my insides are made of glass. This is such a bad idea. 'It's great to see you Aaron.' What do you say to someone you loved three years and half a face ago?

'You don't live above Tops Grocery anymore. I've rung your doorbell a few times.'

This is news. 'Not for a while.'

His phone rings, and from his side of the conversation I gather he lives with his girlfriend, and they share the complexities of domestic cohabitation. It's a far cry from his being shirtless and pantless, standing in my kitchen making cowboy coffee. He's such a grown-up now.

'Sorry about that,' as he shuts off his phone.

'It's all good,' the Black Label and beer and the dying heat are taking effect. Everything is floating.

Aaron laughs to himself. 'I saved that Absolute Ritts ad.'

I don't hide my surprise. 'Why did you ring my ex-doorbell?' Aaron had made me his ex-girlfriend. That Absolut Ritts ad was the beginning of our end.

'I missed you.' He looks at my good side and places his hand over mine. His calluses rub against my knuckles. He must still lift weights. He leans in closer. 'Can I ask what happened?' He smells like the ocean coated with honey.

You can. But answering requires another round. Alat pokes his head into the beer garden. Hold up two fingers and circle them twice. Make mine a double and everything nice.

'I was on a shoot in Marrakesh. We made a last minute stop at the souk. A motorcycle bomb went off.' He waits. 'Near where I was standing.' How much more do I need to explain? Half my face is worth a thousand words.

An eruption of laughter peels through the beer garden.

ALEX POPPE

Aaron leans closer, the beer mixing with the sweet smell of his breath. The sweet breath of a sweet man in a sweet world. 'I'm sorry.' He caresses the top of my hand. 'What do the doctors say?'

What do doctors say about cancelled modelling contracts, about cancelled dreams? I finger my rubber band. Right now, I'd settle for drinks out, hold the stares. It's fucking funny: after a lifetime of look-at-me, I wish I were invisible. What do wishes look like?

'They don't say much.' Which isn't exactly true. They said a lot when I was there this afternoon. They said I could do a ton of plastic surgery and maybe I'd come out looking like a comic book character or maybe like someone I resembled. But not like me. 'I don't want to end up the female equivalent of Mickey Rourke.'

This comment earns me a half-smile. 'Same old Jax.'

Not really.

'There are so many surgical advances today. Don't give up hope.' He sounds like a cross between an inspirational speaker and an infomercial. My hand sweats under his palm. I don't want pity.

'Yeah, you're right. *Face/Off* was practically a documentary.' I take my hand back.

He looks into my good eye. Freeze frame. 'You were so beautiful.'

The world goes silent.

I was a lot of other things too. No one ever saw them.

The smell of sunbaked pavement wafts through the garden. We empty another round as the sun empties from the sky, banding it blue, green, yellow. I need. To touch. I need to fuck. It's weird to miss someone you are sitting with. Aaron has to go. If I could give back three things to make him stay, I'd

GIRL, WORLD

give back vintage champagne, all my stays in luxury hotels, and that Absolut Ritts ad. That ad was everything.

'It was great seeing you Jax.'

Why do I think I will never see him again? 'You too Aaron.' My words are soggy. And just like that, he is gone.

*

I smell it before I see it. Can't see anything behind the big bag of supplies I'm carrying. Was feeling accomplished that I remembered to buy Moxie-necessities on the way home before the smell of dog piss bitch-slapped me across the face when I opened my front door. At least Moxie skirts the puddle instead of running through it. I follow her lead. It's easier than cleaning it.

Moxie noses my calves as I fill her bowl with dog food and set it near her impatient tail. 'Sorry for the wait.' Pour myself a Black Label and sit to watch her eat. Doggie gulping noises permeate the kitchen. 'Slow down girl. A lady picks.' I don't pick. I point. At junk food in supermarkets or bakeries. I look and point and pretend I am going to eat something delicious, something bad for me. Sometimes, looking is enough. At least I'm not a puker like a lot of other models are. I went to the souk that day to look at the dried fruits in the spice market. Wanted to point at rings of pineapple and wedges of mango and garlands of dates. Wanted to pretend I was going to eat them.

Moxie settles herself by my feet. She looks at me with these wide, open eyes. There's a lump pushing up my throat, and I am tempted to kick her. Her blind trust fucking pisses me off. Grabbing my drink, I open the kitchen window to sit on the fire escape. The night hushes.

ALEX POPPE

The sky has gone inky. From its depth, a single star watches. Looking at my reflection in the kitchen window, I see a faceless girl staring back at me. I want to wake up in her body. There's a hard, blank feeling inside me. I should sleep. When I was up-and-comer, I never slept. Didn't want to miss anything. It's different now.

Moxie is asleep on her blanket when I creep back inside. Do dogs dream? Maybe she is dreaming of running through open green spaces, of catching shiny red balls. Tomorrow, I'll take her to the park. Buy her a toy. Remember to feed her.

The sheets are cool as I slip in between them. Fucking hate sleeping alone. I sleep on only half the bed. Used to love it, back in the day when there were a lot of admirers. Back then, I needed the quiet. Now the quiet riots. Rewind and rewrite tonight as my fingertips stroke my stomach. I am not a boyfriend thief, so in my version of reality Aaron does not have a girlfriend whom he lives with. My fingertips tickle up to pinch my nipples. My tits are full, my nipples erect. He says I am beautiful, not was, because he sees past the candy shell. Because he misses parking lot salsa lessons and being read to in the bathtub. My hand slides down. Inside I am smooth and slippery. I roll over and grind my pelvis. Pictures flash – Jeff's cock, sucking Aaron's bottom lip, a rock star's head between my thighs, tongues pushing more and more and more. My pelvis hooks. An extended present tense. I taste the pillow with my grimace. My body slackens. The ability to speak returns. There is the static noise of silence. My pillow smells sad. I miss so much: middle-of-the-day sex and lying face to face sharing a pillow. Fuck, I miss resting my cheek against my hand. The pillowcase irritates. I turn over toward the window. The sky has lightened. Four black birds fly in a diamond formation against a white sky. How

GIRL, WORLD

do they stay together? Even lovebirds get divorced. Flying is a cool superpower, but I would choose instant regeneration. My mouth tastes like how the front hallway smells. Fucking need to take care of the Moxie mess. Like now. I am on my hands and knees with paper towel and dog piss soaked journal pages before breakfast. Living the life. Fuck, I miss maid service. That was a great perk of living in model apartments. The agency puts five young hopefuls in a too small space, competing for the same jobs, and expects them not to kill each other. There is always an odd number of housemates: provides a built-in moderator. I lived in one in Paris. Between the hair-pulling and the tears there were some moments.

Vive Le Paris! Jeff came over for a visit. All the other girls are like mad in love with him. Who wouldn't be? He's like totally hot and nice and cool and 24! Plus, French Vogue *just hired him. And he likes ME! He says he like "discovered me" and he's real proud of it. Mom would FREAK if she heard that because she was my first agent. Anyway, I don't care because it's summer, and I'm in PARIS, and the night sky goes on forever, and I'm in love!!! I haven't said it yet or anything because I'm not like totally stupid, but it's love.*

On Friday nights parades of people skate around the Canal Saint Martin. We usually watch them from our balcony. Zaina and Elena (Zaina is from Beirut and has the best hair. Elena is from Kiev and is the skinniest.) got booked on the same shoot and bought us all blades! (They had ten pages of editorial for Italian Elle! *Jealous☹) I haven't scored anything as big, but I feel like it's coming. On Monday I have a go-see for some Pirelli calendar. Whoever that is. Anyway, we drank some Voov Cli Co champagne, donned our skates, and off we went. It was electric. The*

ALEX POPPE

five of us held hands as we skated, a daisy chain of pretty girls. Nobody was elbowing each other out. I feel like we'll be friends forever.
    But the really big news is this. Wait for it☺. Jeff and I. Hee hee hee. I was really scared because I knew it would hurt, but Jeff was really gentle and patient and like showed me what to do. I was so embarrassed that I didn't know, but I think he got off on that. That he could mold me the way he wanted. I finally feel like I belong to someone.

Jesus Fuck.

There is the clip-clip-clip of tiny paws behind me. The soles of my feet receive a tongue bath. 'Morning Toe Licker,' Picking up Moxie, I breathe my dragon breath in her face. She barks. 'Let's go buy a ball.'

Fuck, that sun is bright. Moxie has decided to take her morning dump in front of the entrance to the Brooklyn Fleas. She has no shame. Of course not. She's not the one bent over, picking up warm, squishy dog shit with a sandwich baggie.

'Jax! I'd recognize you anywhere,' a voice addresses my ass. 'Girl when did you get a dog? You can barely take care of yourself.'

Turning around, I spy Frieda's locks before I spy Frieda. Everything on Frieda has been added: hair, fingernails, breasts. She's a trannie makeup artist with an identical twin brother named Frank. I wonder how long it took for their mother to stop calling 'Boys…' when she wanted both of them. 'Yesterday. This is Moxie. Moxie meet Aunt Frieda.' Frieda's one of my few before and after friends.

'How you feelin?' She takes my chin and turns my face to look at both sides. Her silver bangles jangle. 'Did you see the doctor I told you about?'

She gets away with touching my face because of her six

GIRL, WORLD

inch height advantage. And because she was on that Marrakesh shoot. 'Yeah. Yesterday.' I wriggle free. She was at the airport at the time of the blast. She visited me almost every week during my recovery to give me a mani/pedi. No one asked her to.

'Girl, you look like shit. Even for you.'

Can't argue with that.

'When's the last time you ate?'

'This morning.'

'Liar.'

She's right. 'So don't ask.' I get indignant when I'm called out.

'Want to have brunch?'

'Can't. I have shit to do.'

'Right. Like you're so important.' Frieda never sugarcoats it.

'Fuck you. I have to get Moxie a ball.'

'So get her a ball after. Girl, starving yourself to death is going to take a while. ODing is much quicker.'

'Fuck you. I don't starve myself.' Besides, I've already decided on hanging. If I were to.

'Fuck you.' Frieda sounds like a junior high cheerleader. 'Fuck you.'

I don't sound that whiny.

'Fuck you-ou.' Frieda's bopping about as she sings it. 'Fuck youuu. Hoo-hooooo. You can push me away all you like.' Frieda grabs my hands and makes me dance along with her. 'But I'm not going anywhere, you dumb, skinny bitch.' She snaps my rubber band. 'Class bling. Let's go to Meatballs. You can drink your lunch. Like Moxie, I need me some balls in my mouth.' Frieda's laugh sounds like a delicious secret.

ALEX POPPE

Bending down to ruffle Moxie's fur, I hide my smile. Sometimes it's easier to give in.

❋

After brunch, liquid and otherwise, Moxie and I stroll through McCarren Park. Frieda has a date. Dating – more like snacking. I don't know why Frieda appointed herself my fairy godmother, but I am grateful. She's hooked me up for a prop styling gig next week, which is lucky because I need something to do.

What the fuck am I going to do with the rest of my life?

Me: *Hi. Is this Lost and Found? I've lost my way.*

Lost and Found: *Have you checked the places you were? You probably left it there.*

Me: *I can't go back to where I was. They won't let me in. I'm not beautiful anymore.*

Lost and Found: *I know. Look, it'll turn up. I always find my iPhone at the wine bar across from my apartment.*

Me: *Can you just look? It's shiny gold and leads to the top.*

Lost and Found: *Aren't you special? Those are one in a million. Yeah, no. It's not here. You should have taken better care of it in the first place.*

Me: *But, it's not my fault it's gone.*

Lost and Found: *Isn't it?*

Me: *Look, do you know where I can buy a new one?*

Lost and Found: *Do I look like Information? Kindly step aside Ma'am. You're holding up the line.*

Shit. My rubber band is gone. That bitch must have lifted it during the "Fuck You" dance. Despite her Emily Post posture, Frieda's always had sticky fingers.

GIRL, WORLD

An African drum ensemble starts up on the far side of the park grabbing Moxie's attention. She's strong when she wants her way. A small group of people gather around the musicians, dancing. I recognize Jules playing a modest drum near the center of the cluster. Jules is a protest artist whose big moment came when Jay Z bought one of his paintings. That moment went. Jules' hands slap the drum skin, his long, thick fingers splayed. Feeling a tickle rise between my legs causes me to look away from his lapping fingers. I dated Jules for a minute a lifetime ago.

'Hey pretty, do you want to dance?' An unfamiliar voice calls from my good side. Turning toward it, I hear a muffled gasp. 'Sorry, thought you were someone else.' He flees.

Fuck you asshole. I'd rather dance with my dog.

※

Back home, I feed Moxie and sit with my friend Johnnie Walker. I need to kiss someone in the worst way. To put all of who I am into lips and tongue and touch. Kissing is underrated because it's all about the before. People rush that. They don't get that kissing is hope.

Who am I kidding? I need to lose myself in a good lay. Shut out thought and time and place for however long intense foreplay and a heroic orgasm lasts. I swear, I am ready to call an escort service and order a totally hot guy who stares not and sexes sweet. Not like the last hookup who grabbed a pillow to smother me as I came, and then squirted in my face as he lifted the pillow. I choked and he laughed. Like I wasn't a real person. To him, I was only the shape of one. I don't expect breakfast, but some people are too rough to fuck. It's a fine line deciding whose standards are low enough. Like it

ALEX POPPE

fucking matters. In the dark you become whomever they want. Then in the end, you're left with who you are. Jesus mother fucking Christ! I can't stand it inside my head.

With nowhere to go, I go to Alat's.

Sans Moxie, I sit at the air-conditioned bar and watch Alat work. He doesn't say much to anyone. He's probably killed people. How he does not drink the entire contents of the bar baffles me.

'I feel you watching me.' Alat has his back to me polishing glasses. Must be his child soldier instincts kicking in.

'No I'm not.' I smile like a receptionist at his back.

'Why are you always here alone?' He picks up a knife and starts cutting lemons.

'I'm not always alone. Yesterday I had Moxie.' And Aaron, sort of. 'You're always here alone. Why doesn't your girlfriend ever visit you?' Figure girlfriend is the safer bet.

'My wife is at home with our sons.' Eights words tell me more about him than half as many months of patronage. Where's his ring? 'Muslim women do not usually frequent bars.' Who knew he was religious?

'Did you meet her in Brooklyn?'

'No.'

'Did you know her from Somalia?'

'She knows about my past.'

'That's not what I was asking.' Of course I deny it.

'Then what?'

That lump is back, clogging my throat. What I really want to know is how he put himself back together. Half-true. I want to know how to put myself back together. Johnnie Walker isn't telling.

'Jax, it's time to grow up. You've had so much more than

GIRL, WORLD

most.' Alat's eyes are shiny; his voice is not unkind. 'Beauty doesn't feed you.'

Uh, in my case it did.

'How you look can't sustain you here,' Alat's hand covers his heart. 'Become the person you are supposed to be.'

I have no idea who that is. I used to be so many people.

✤

Twilight hugs the buildings as I walk Moxie along the Williamsburg Bridge. The sky swirls cornflower to carnation as it races the horizon. Looking at it makes my heart hurt in a good way. There is so much beauty above; it makes me feel the tiniest bit alive. The sky was like this in Marrakesh. A color frenzy served up nightly. Thinking about that last day is like touching a hot stove. I last for only so long. It had been my idea to go to the souk. The handler said we needed to get to the airport. I insisted. People don't usually say no to pretty girls.

Purple clouds reef over the East River. All across the boroughs, pretty girls self-decorate and preen in this city of dreams. A leashed figure on four legs pulls a straining figure on two legs around the bottom of Bedford Avenue and heads in our direction. A voice tells Woody to slow down, to heel, but Woody isn't having it. He must have caught Moxie's scent. The two-legged figure turns out to be Heather, a local jewelry designer and sometimes stylist. Jeff bought me one of her pieces, and when I found out about him and Elena (Jax, I zwear it meant nothink. I only did him to get into the *Vogue*), I threw it into the Seine.

Woody reaches his destination and tries to sniff Moxie. She barks and moves away, playing hard to get. But when

I reach down to pet him, she charges nose first into his ass. He lets her. Then he tries to mount her. Shit-fuck! I haven't checked if Moxie's been spayed.

'Jax! What a coincidence.' Heather calls as she restrains Woody. 'You're working with me next week. I didn't know you have a dog. Frieda didn't say when we spoke.'

Fairy godmother Frieda must have prepped Heather on my condition because my face doesn't faze her. 'That's great. Frieda didn't give me the specifics.' Sometimes Brooklyn feels like a village.

'It'll be easy. *Interview* magazine. New York City writers and artists. We probably already have lots of the required items in our personal collections. I'll email you the list.'

People always assume models have tons of shit. When you're starting out, you get paid in merchandise. As you make a name, you get paid in money, a lot of which winds up your nose. Truth is, we wear "borrowed" so often there's no need to buy. *Was* no need to buy. 'I'll look through what I have.'

'Some of us are going to Brooklyn Bowl tonight. There's some Portland band. You should come.'

*

After Marrakesh I decided it was best not to look at my whole face in the mirror. When I brush my teeth, I usually walk around the apartment dripping toothpaste. If I apply makeup, I parcel my features in a hand mirror. The full-length mirror is propped against the bedroom wall at neck height. Johnnie Walker has encouraged me to try something new. I sneak up on the bathroom.

Don't be such a pussy. Lights on. Fuck, just look at yourself. When you were sixteen you stared into everything reflective.

GIRL, WORLD

Count of three. Go. Seeing the caulked texture of my dark cheek causes a hot stripe to shoot up my throat. Scabby spackle tracks my right temple and fans above my right eyebrow. Widening my scope, I take in my straight nose and generous mouth. Breathe. My eyes sweep left and up. Dewy, creamy, porcelain skin. Finally I meet my gaze. Stagnant eyes regard me.

Johnnie Walker you are a tricking, Tom-fuckery, son of a bitch. The only response is to finish you.

My handler leads me through the souk's labyrinth of stalls. The scents of jasmine and orange blossom flirt with the aroma of chicken shish. Everywhere is Color! Color! Color! Barrels of mustard yellow saffron, burnt sienna turmeric, and dried red peppers compete with three foot Crayola hued flowers under a candy blue sky. Somewhere an oud plays. My mouth waters for the dried pineapple and mango which hang in slabs above the barrels. The fruit slabs have hinged jaws, which start moving up and down laughing. Their dried-strawberry kebab tongues lash at my hair. I point at the slabs while my handler negotiates the price. 'No,' my lips move as if in peanut butter. I can't form words. My handler turns toward me. Everything quiets to a vibration as a motorcycle pauses down the lane. The vibration grows to a rumble to a thunder to silence as the motorcycle cartwheels apart. A hubcap frisbees through the air. The ground hits me. My face feels like wet fire. Some god unmutes the sound. Under invocations and pounding footsteps, there is doglike moaning flooding with saliva. A siren wails and wails and wails.

The ringing phone wakes me. How the fuck did I end up on the bathroom floor? Stop ringing stop ringing stop ringing. Silence. Thank you oh merciful God. My mouth tastes like dry, cracked ass. The bathroom sink helps me stand. The room swivels from side to side. Fucking phone starts fucking ringing again. Jesus fuck, who the hell calls at 3:00 a.m.? It's not like I have fucking fuck buddies. Stumble into the kitchen. No phone but there is a scatter of dog chow on the floor and a snoring Moxie. Her legs move as if she's running. The ringing stops while I pop some aspirin and starts again by the time I dump the contents of my handbag onto the living room floor to find my phone.

'Frieda, what the fuck. It's after three.' I feel vomity.

'Girl, where's "hello"? Didn't your mama raise you right?'

Emily Post manners too.

'She raised me not to fucking phone at three in the fucking morning. Look, if this is about–'

'Girl, it's not all about you. I need you.'

FUCK.

'What happened?'

'Just come over.'

What could be a few minutes later, I am panting outside Frieda's apartment door.

'Girl, is that what you sleep in? No wonder you're attracting degenerates.'

I should have never told her about the Smother-Squirter.

'What, no half-smart, full-of-fucks response? Do I look that bad?'

She does. Her left eye is swollen shut and her bottom lip is split. Her wig lies forgotten near the sofa. Her open kimono exposes her hairless flat chest and swollen, knobby ribs. Her upper thighs look like they have been kicked a thousand times. I go into the kitchen to avoid looking at her and come back with some fresh ice. Frieda's lying on the couch examining her face in a hand mirror. Most of her fingernails have been broken.

GIRL, WORLD

'Girl, is that all you got? Ice? You? That is downright shameful. Go get Mama a tequila. It's much more to the point.' Her voice trails me into the kitchen. 'Bring the bottle.'

'Do you want to go to the hospital? I'll go with you.'

Frieda's right eye cuts me.

I hand her a shot. 'What happened? I thought you had a date.'

'It's all fun and games until somebody gets laid. Bastard ran first sign of trouble.'

'I'm sorry.' What else is there to say? I refresh her ice packs and get her a blanket and another pillow. Take the mirror from her hands. 'Trust me. You don't need this now.' Put some ointment on Frieda's split lip and gently wipe her lone tear. Her right eye watches as I pull a chair up to the sofa and settle in for what's left of the night. Her knuckles interlace mine as her breathing deepens into slumber.

I wake to wet. My forehead is resting on damp sofa cushions next to Frieda's stomach. All the ice packs have melted. Some fucking nurse I am. Untangle my hand from Frieda's and head to the kitchen to mix some tequila and OJ for her. She's going to hurt when she wakes.

'Girl, what are you doing in my kitchen? Lord knows you don't know how to cook.'

'Mixing a magic potion. Here. Drink this. Then I'll help you shower.'

Frieda wrinkles her nose like I've just farted garlic and cheese. 'Help me what? No.'

'For fuck's sake Frieda. It's not like I haven't seen one before.'

'But mine is spectacular.' She dirty laughs and grabs near her ribs. 'I don't want to ruin you.'

'Little late for that. Cheers.'

ALEX POPPE

'Shit girl.' Frieda coughs hard. 'Is the juice just for color?'
'You need to numb yourself. You think you hurt now? You're not even standing.' Frieda takes my comment as a challenge and swings her legs round to the floor, biting back a groan. She settles back and drains her drink. We wait for the tequila effect.
   'Are you scared?'
   'Scared of little boys with little pricks and even littler minds? Shit no, girl. Bring it on.' Her face says anything but. With all the wrappings torn away, Frieda looks like someone who's kept one eye over her shoulder her whole life.
   'Ready for your sponge bath? It'll be fun.'
   'You ever bathe someone? Medically speaking?'
   'No, but I once sucked Jeff off as some guy popped his dislocated shoulder back into its socket. Does that count?' Am I exaggerating? Mostly.
   Frieda can't tell whether to believe me or not. 'To think all this time, I thought you were a good girl.'
   'More like a good slut.' I hold out both my hands to Frieda and gently pull her up.

❊

   By the time I get home, Moxie has peed the floor again. Can't really blame her. Thank God for Bounty, the quicker picker-upper. I wish they made the equivalent for people.
   As Moxie eats I reach for my laptop instead of Johnnie Walker. Seeing Frieda all beat up is fucking with me.
   Heather's email is at the top. Scan her prop list. A bullwhip? Really? She'd be better off asking Frieda. Gothic jewelry? Check. Will bring that Peruzzi cross. Hot house orchids? Curious to see who these artists will be. About to

GIRL, WORLD

log off when a new message pings my inbox.

The name is Arabic so I know who it's from before I open it. Get up and am halfway to the shelf where Johnny Walker lives when the image of Frieda's right eye watching me doctor her cut lip pushes into my mind. Her dirty laugh echoes in my empty kitchen. Motionless I stand listening to Moxie's paws clacking against the tiles. Snap. My wrist smarts. Snap. I go back to my chair and sit down. Mr. Walker's not going anywhere.

Dear Miss Jax,

I hope you is well and your family. I write you for to show you how Layla growing. Me attache the image. The money that you us gave it when Naji was died very help us. Ma Layla in the school. She and me in security. She and me, we have good life.

As-salaam 'alaykum,
Aamina El-Khoury

Aamina was my handler's wife. His name was Naji. Naji. I almost never say it. Not even in my mind. Refer to him as The Handler. But he had a name. And a wife. And a daughter. Then a dervish motorcycle hubcap spun into his neck and he didn't have them anymore. That moment lives in my head, an always. Condolence payments didn't bring him back. Another thing you can't buy. I pick up Moxie to show her the sweet picture of Layla. Bury my face in her fur. She smells alive. My growling stomach startles us both.

Moxie and I head over to Teddy's Bar and Grill under a dirty sky. Teddy's serves a tequila sampler in case Frieda

ALEX POPPE

checks her messages and joins us. I sit at an outside table to watch the world go by as Moxie settles at my feet. Thinking about Aamina's email and the prop gig tomorrow makes me feel lighter. I order a goat cheese burger.

The smell of weed wafts by. It's followed by a tall, skinny dude with dark chin-length hair and a high forehead. His ears are pierced, his goatee trimmed, and his green eyes red. There is something about him that makes me want to wear leather and run out to get my nipples pierced and my ass tattooed. Even Moxie is distracted from the lure of my toes by this stranger's entrance. Fucking why-oh-why did I wear a lavender sundress? I feel like a reject from a prom dress casting. Shit. He just caught me staring. Shitty fuck. I have nothing to hide behind.

'Hey,' he passes and sits down at the next table. I "hey" back wondering how high he is not to have been freaked out by my face. It's not like I can turn around to check.

'My Lord girl, is that you in a dress?'

Frieda knows how to make an entrance. She has styled herself like an Amazonian Holly Golightly in oversized dark sunglasses and a little black shift. She sports a diamante clip in her streaked updo and pearls around her neck. 'Glad to see you're feeling better.' I stand and awkwardly hug her. Moxie barks her approval.

'Girl, you know you can't keep a good woman down. Not unless she wants to be, and you've been a veeery good.' Frieda laughs like I've offered her a Cartier box filled with diamonds and then winces, fingering her ribs. Swagger tromps pain. The waitress appears with my burger. 'Now I've seen it all.'

'I told you I eat.' Just not every day. 'It's not my fucking fault you fucking don't believe me. Want half?'

GIRL, WORLD

'Thank God that sentence had at least one "fuck" in it or I'd doubt you were you.'

'No one else has this face.'

'No one else has that body either. And right now it is being admired by one very sexy stoner.' Frieda leans back. 'Hey-hey at the next table. Were you just checking out my friend's very fine ass?'

I'm ready to stuff my burger in her mouth. A chair scrapes along the sidewalk. Way to go Frieda. Frighten the poor fucker away.

A low chuckle. 'I guess I was.' His voice invites like a bowl of hot chocolate.

'I can't say I blame you,' Frieda says, lowering her sunglasses. 'It's even better bare,' she purrs.

Jesus mother fucking Christ. 'Shut the fuck up!' I hiss, breaking the cinematic inevitability of the moment.

'What? Do you feel objectified?' Frieda deep throats one of my French fries. 'Are you, the model of *the* Absolut Ritts ad and two *Sports Illustrated Swimsuit Issue* covers, offended by compliments to your physique?' It is awe inspiring and a little gross what Frieda's tongue does with food. 'Besides, I think he's enjoying the attention. His Christmas eyes are smiling.'

I shrug my eyebrows in response.

Frieda flags the browsing waitress. 'You don't understand. You've never been background music.'

'But now I'm a fucking freak show.'

'Even the Elephant Man got laid.'

'Frieda, I'm serious. I miss what I looked like, and I don't care how shallow that sounds.'

'You're more than what you look like.'

When did Frieda become cliché?

ALEX POPPE

'No I'm not. None of us are. Look at you. You got the shit kicked out of you last night and today you're peacocking.'

'I may decorate the outside but I know what's inside. Despite the cock and balls, I am one hundred percent woman.' Frieda sings the last word over to Christmas Eyes, smiling with all her teeth.

'You go through a lot of work to be a *pretty* woman. Just last night all those fingernails were broken. Today, good as new. Because life is easier for pretty people.' Frieda was out with me enough before Marrakesh to know this is true. How many times did we get VIP treatment or some impossible freebie because of how I looked?

'Girl, that's trappings. They're not beauty and they don't last. What would you have done when you got old?'

I don't know. 'Wait for my professional athlete/rock star husband to cheat on me while I raise our kids upstate? Isn't that what supermodels do?' Truth is, I never thought past the next booking. Before Marrakesh, the bookings seemed like they'd last forever.

'Do you want children? You know, they're harder than dogs.' Her comment stops my feeding Moxie bits of my burger.

Doesn't motherhood have a learning curve? 'I know I am supposed to.'

'Your problem is you don't know what you want.'

'Yes I do. I want my old life back. It was so easy. Someone told me where to be and when to be there, and all I had to do was show up and live in whatever created fantasy there was while someone took my picture. Who wouldn't want that?'

'Not everyone. That life is lonely.'

'All life is lonely. That's why people breed.'

Frieda shakes her head. 'That's not why you have

GIRL, WORLD

children. Anyway, that part of your life is over.'
Looking back is prettier than looking at. 'But I like life through the looking glass.'
'You're whining.'
She's right.
We sip in silence.

*

The thought's pestering me like a roving itch. When I was beautiful, was I happy? Most of the time, I was moving too fast to be anything. It was fun, but is fun the same as happy? It's been eight months since Marrakesh and I don't remember how happy feels.

Moxie and I walk the waterfront desire line of Kent Avenue toward the Brooklyn Navy Yard. I love this old, mixed neighborhood with its industrial buildings and scarred city-scape. It's that hour of daylight when you wish you could taste sunshine. A starvation-zone body of a girl, modeling portfolio under her arm, scurries toward the Domino Sugar Refinery. She has my hair and eyes, and if I were twelve years younger and just starting out, we'd probably run into each other at the same casting calls. What gets me is her gait; she hasn't taken charge of herself. She'll need to own it if she wants to walk New York, Paris, or Milan.

A beeping horn startles me. What the fuck? A truck painted with Hayman's Handyman Service pulls up alongside me. Christmas Eyes is behind the wheel.

'Hey.'

He likes his one syllable words.

'Hey.' Moxie and I approach the truck. 'What's Hayman's Handyman Service?'

ALEX POPPE

'It's pronounced *high* man and it's my company.'
Hymen? I smother a smile. 'What's your first name?'
'Richard.'
He is straight-faced. It is too much. I have to go there.
'So your parents named you 'Richard Hymen, Dick Hymen. Do you still talk to them?'
'It sounds different in Hebrew. Do you want a ride?'
'I'm walking Moxie. Riding defeats the purpose.'
'I have a dog near Prospect Park. We could walk them together.'
'How fast can you move? Usually we shit and run.'
'That's not cool.'
A stoner with a conscience.
'I know,' I say as my hand puppetizes the plastic baggie at the bottom of my handbag. Emerging, the bag takes on a voice of its own. 'Feed me,' it growls.
'You're crazy.' He opens the passenger side door and I climb in, with a stranger who is totally high. Crazy is a sliding scale.
'What's your name?'
'Jax.'
'And you busted *my* balls?'
'My name is cool.'
'I'm sure "Jax" is on your birth certificate.'
'It is!' I lie. I don't cop to Jacinda.
Holding Moxie on my lap, I tell the kind of stories you tell someone who has no idea who you are. I wonder when he'll realize that most of it is bullshit. I'd love to know if he's high enough to sex me. You think about what someone's like when you first meet him.
We pull up to your average, pre-gentrified neighborhood triplex. 'This is me.' He parks.

GIRL, WORLD

I am suddenly nervous about leaving the front seat. This whole time, he's faced my left side. 'Do you want to get your dog while I wait here?' I watch his slim hips walk away.

Free from the truck, Moxie runs her crazy-dog circles around me. A moment later Richard returns with an ambling tobacco-colored mutt. How much weed does he smoke inside his apartment?

'This is Dean.' Richard bends down to rub Dean's head and neck. He pauses to check the milky film over Dean's right eye and whispers something I can't hear in Dean's ear. Then he steps aside to let the dogs meet. Moxie approaches Dean and sniffs. Dean couldn't care less. Moxie barks and barks at Dean's staggering indifference. Dean turns away to follow Richard.

'That went well. Which way to the park?'

'Follow me.' Richard doesn't bother leashing Dean.

I stay on his right side so from his point of view it seems like everyone walking dogs has a normal face.

When we get to the park, I unleash Moxie. She sniffs at every tree while Dean trails us like an Italian chaperone. 'How old is he?'

'Dean's eleven. What about Moxie?'

I don't know. 'I got her from an animal shelter a few days ago. This dog thing is a bit new for me.'

'Why'd you get her?'

'It's like...you know.' My answer satisfies stoner logic. 'Why'd you stop me on Kent?'

'I was leaving my dealer's and I thought, there's that girl with the very fine ass.'

'What about the face?' I keep my gaze on the horizon. The light has gone pastel.

'Less fine than your ass.' His answer is an emotional

ALEX POPPE

paper cut. 'What happened?'

'Wrong place, wrong time.' I decide to flirt with hurt. 'Do you think a person could ever not notice it?'

He stops walking and turns me toward him. Because little jolts of electricity twist from his fingertips up my arms, I indulge his looking spree. His gaze is honest but not reproachful. My stomach unclenches. 'No. It's hard to look at and hard not to.'

Skin crackling silence.

'Being high helps.'

What are the chances he's high all the time?

'Your friends notice it, but they know you so they probably don't care.'

I think about Frieda. She treats me the same as always. When Heather invited me to Brooklyn Bowl, she didn't seem to care. That dancing asshole in the park cared. Did Aaron care?

'You could always drink at vet halls if you don't want it stared at. Next to a serious burn victim, your face would seem minor.'

Comparative attractive suffering – the new reality TV show.

'You don't say much.'

'I'm thinking about what you've said.' It feels like he's shown me the stranger of myself. Am I supposed to be thankful? Does his rock star appeal outweigh his assholeness? Will he suggest I write to prison convicts next?

'I've seen worse.'

I pull a smile out from some place. Get it right on the second try. It pisses me off when people remind me that others have suffered more than I have. They didn't lose what I lost. Where?'

'When I was in the army in Israel.'

GIRL, WORLD

'What'd you do?'

'If a bomb went off or there was a firefight, I was on the team that removed the damaged vehicles. We worked near the Lebanese border. We were busy.'

'I was on a shoot in Marrakesh. Insisted on going to the souk. There was a motorcycle bomb.' Those tumultuous, stupid seconds. 'In a way, it's my own fucking fault.'

'No it's not. Bomb shit is uncool. Grew up with that shit.'

Being a product of privileged America, my words go into hiding.

'Dude, where's your dog?'

Shit-fuck. It's been a while since I've seen or heard Moxie. Dean sits at Richard's feet like a testament to Richard's abilities as a pet owner. I thrust the empty dog leash inside my handbag.

'Don't worry. We'll find her.'

I envy his cannabis calm.

'Moxie!' I yell as I run forward. 'Moxie, I've got your red ball. Moxie! Toe Licker. Come out, come out wherever you are!' The fucking trees sing back to me.

Mother-ass bitch! Why can't I enjoy a fucking walk in the park like a normal fucking person without losing my fucking dog? Frieda's right. I can't take care of myself. Who was I fooling getting a dog? I've never kept houseplants. I'm incapable of sustaining anything lasting.

I hear Richard yelling for Moxie in another part of the park. Tree shadows tickle the shrubs as the sun climbs down from the sky. I feel violent toward the park. What looks to be a seven-year-old boy pokes a stick at something under a giant oak. He frolics with the boughs, his mop of curly red hair bobbing up and down as if the leaves answer him. His loose laughter makes me want to slap the joy right out of him.

ALEX POPPE

Snap. Snap. Snap. The pain jolts. Snap. My feet move toward him unearthing grasslings. Snap. Maybe he's seen Moxie.

'Whatcha got there?'

Startled, the boy straightens, brandishing the stick like a sword. When he sees my face, he screams and runs helter-skelter, disappearing within the folds of the park's leafy skirt. 'I'm gonna get you. I'm gonna get you. I'm gonna get you.' My voice scratches like jagged tree bark. Fucking brat. Walking fucking argument for birth control. Wish I could fucking shove him back up his mother's hooch. Where he was standing is a brown, chunky puddle with bits of ground pinky sirloin.

Richard and Dean catch up to me. Dean's presence is an accusation. 'Any luck?'

'Maybe. Is that animal or human?'

Richard restrains Dean. 'The way Dean's interested I would say animal. It could be dog puke or diarrhea. Did you feed her any of your lunch?'

I had ordered today's goat cheese burger medium rare. 'How did you know to come this way?'

'Some screaming kid ran past me. Figured he might have seen you.'

'Fuck you.'

Richard shrugs his shoulders as he hands me a business card. 'Email me a picture of Moxie with contact info, and I'll put up some fliers in the neighborhood. Someone might have taken her home.'

I don't have a single picture of Moxie. I couldn't make a fucking missing dog flyer if I wanted to. I take his card. The sky looks tenuous. Did I say thank you? 'She's probably better off without me.'

'Don't be like that. I've seen the ways she licks your feet. You'll find her.' He squeezes my shoulder. 'Look, I need to

GIRL, WORLD

get Dean home to give him his eye drops. If you follow the path to the right, it leads toward the lake. Does she like water? Maybe you'll find her there. If you don't find her, send me that picture.' He and Dean head left into the shadows. Our paths diverge like two people who go back to their separate lives.

Kurdistan

I am fifteen years old. My parents are dead. I have a blue bird puppet named Annie made out of that fake fur they use for fuzzy pencils in my carry-on bag, and a copy of *To Kill a Mockingbird* in my lap. The heavy-set woman next to me keeps offering me Oreo cookies from the pointy black purse balanced on her belly. There is chocolate dust around the corners of her mouth but I don't have the nerve to tell her. Instead, I look out the window of the plane and see a shadow girl staring back at me.

I am moving to Kurdistan. Most Americans think Kurdistan is Kyrgyzstan unless they are from Nashville or San Diego where a lot of Kurdish people live. Those people know Kurdistan is in Northern Iraq. They know it has mountains. And green parts. And oil.

Aunt Maya is waiting for me outside the security checkpoint. Her blue headscarf is bedazzled. Red hair peeks out from the sides. She hugs me the same way Mom used to – hands pressing both sides of my face– and asks if I remember her. Through squeezed cheeks I pucker yes and breathe in Shalimar. I want to take Annie out of my carry-on, but I know I am too old to play with her in public.

This part of Kurdistan doesn't look green. It's brown and dusty. Aunt Maya leads me to a gleaming white Land Cruiser. I wonder how she keeps the dust off. Her driver takes my bags. He wears mirrored sunglasses and a dark

GIRL, WORLD

suit with a dark tie. Aunt Maya and I sit in the back. The car smells like her perfume and new plastic. There is an odd-looking rifle poking up from the floor of the front seat.

The highway leading from the airport is dotted with parked cars. Whole families with mothers and fathers and daughters picnic at the side of the road. Women in long colorful dresses sit on brown grass around open fires. The men wear what look like a brown onesie belted with a wide sash. They remind me of feet pajamas. As we drive, a fiery sun sinks down and divides the sky into a band of blue squashing a band of orange to conquer the horizon. We pass clusters of identical new homes that look like they have been cut from raw cookie dough. There is a mall with amusement park rides. A roller coaster towers behind a sign announcing "Family Land".

Aunt Maya asks, You have Family Land in Tennessee?

It takes me a moment to figure out what she means. Then I see her looking at the sign. I tell her we have malls, but not with roller coasters.

She says, I take you.

It is hilly and my ears haven't adjusted from the plane. I squeeze my nose and exhale. It doesn't work. Every sound comes to me from underwater. We pass a gated compound with orange buildings. There are soldiers at the entrance with the same odd-looking rifles as the driver. In front of the gate is a collapsible grate with jagged metal teeth. Aunt Maya points and tells me that is my new school.

We pass a big fancy hotel on a hill across from a field where sheep are grazing. Fuzzy gray bleeds into fuzzy white. We turn right into a compound called American Village. All the houses are big-big. Uniformed guards circle the car, sticking long, shiny mirrored shovels under it. I don't know what they are looking for. We pass inspection and enter.

ALEX POPPE

We pull up to a cookie-dough mansion with white Grecian pillars. The garage juts outward onto the front lawn. Aunt Maya squeezes my arm. We're home.

Around the side of the house the backyard unfolds into a patio palace. A marble dance floor holds court between an outdoor fireplace made of the same marble-y stone and a high-tech DJ station. Adjacent to the fireplace is a sitting area with thick-cushioned couches and a full bar. Our old apartment would fit onto half the patio.

Aunt Maya sees me staring and asks if I'm ok. Her big eyes shine like glass. I don't have the right words so I smile with closed lips. My smile forms a tight line. I tight-line smile a lot these days. The right words don't exist. I would need to invent a whole new language.

❊

Both died in cars. Back home in Tennessee, Mom was at an intersection by a mosque when a bomb went off. She wasn't wearing her seatbelt. Dad was an interpreter for the US Army in Iraq, and he died when his car drove over an IED. He was wearing a seatbelt. What are the chances? Chance is like one of those black scorpions that blindly stings anything that gets in its path. Mom got stung last month. Dad got stung eight years ago.

Mom and Dad were the only ones in their families to emigrate to the US when Saddam was killing Kurds. Now they are gone and Saddam is gone, so the lawyers thought I should go there, here, to be with family. All my relatives are here. Aunt Maya is Mom's sister and she was married to a government minister and that's probably why her house is so big.

Inside it's like a museum. There are paintings behind

GIRL, WORLD

thick glass in gold curlicue frames. The porcelain tiles feel cold under my bare feet. Aunt Maya leads me past a woman stuffing meat and rice into hollowed peppers in the kitchen, upstairs to a bedroom, and all I think is I'm going to get lost in this house. French doors open onto a pink and white room with thick plush carpet. The room smells like almonds and fresh paint. My two oversized suitcases are huddled in the corner. From the doorway, I see their frayed edges. Hopefully, Aunt Maya doesn't see them too. On the dresser is a cloth framed photograph of two girls in long water-colored gowns. Rhinestones cascade down their dress fronts and jitterbug onto their hijabs. Red hair peeks out from the sides of their head scarves.

    I picture Mom in her skinny jeans jumping up to play air guitar whenever her favorite songs were on the radio. Next, she's in a vintage rock T-shirt drinking milk out of the carton when she thought no one was looking. I have never seen her wear a head scarf.

    As soon as Aunt Maya leaves Annie comes out of my carry-on. She's smushed from being packed for so long. With my hand inside her yellow felt beak, she comes to life. Holding her close, I inhale her dusty synthetic odor. She tells me to let her go so she can investigate the room. I make Annie kiss me and feel the cold metal of her beak ring against my lip. Mom pierced her beak to show me it didn't hurt before I got my ears pierced on my tenth birthday.

    Inside the walk-in closet, a row of empty hangers confronts Annie and me. We fall down under them. I have been steamrolled. All the air leaves my chest and I can't swallow. The carpet itches my cheek but I can't scratch it. I can't move. I stare directly into Annie's crossed eyes until I become cross-eyed too. We are both two dimensional. Putting all my concentration

ALEX POPPE

into breathing, I will my lungs to beat like a bird's wings flapping. Gradually, I puff myself back into shape.

*

At 5:02, the call to prayer breaks the morning silence. The plaintive sound reminds me of a coffee commercial. Dusty brown hills meet the low-hanging sky outside my bedroom window. All the colors are washed out in the filmy air. Somewhere a rooster crows.

My stomach growls, but I am chicken to go to the kitchen and help myself. Annie finally dares me into action. I tiptoe down the stairs, take a wrong turn, and end up in the library. The books look old. All the titles are in Kurdish. I make out only a few words. Some have Aunt Maya's surname running along the sides. Outside the library window, the driver is washing Aunt Maya's car. Long, bumpy scars the color of bacon fat crisscross the back of his upper arms and shoulders, disappearing beneath his sleeveless tee. The woman who was preparing food yesterday brings him a mug. Her hand lingers on his forearm. Watching her retrace her steps helps me find my way to the kitchen.

She is making smoothies and doesn't hear me above the whirl of the blender. She uses her right shoulder to itch her cheek without breaking her smoothie-making stride. She has a blister-size mole on the side of her cheek and I wonder if her shoulder feels it. There are lines pulling down the corners of her mouth. She could be anywhere from 30 to 50. She turns and is startled. She points to the blender and says something in Kurdish. I nod my head and she hands me a glass. She smells like a just-opened can of Campbell's Chicken Noodle soup.

GIRL, WORLD

She looks at me and waits. I don't know what I am supposed to do. I want to take the smoothie and run back to my room, but I don't want to be rude. I finish it in one gulp and walk my glass over to the sink. She fires out something in Kurdish and grabs for the glass. Maybe she doesn't want me to wash it out. I tell her it's ok, I don't mind. She is surprisingly strong and won't let go of it. Together, we carry the glass to the sink. I don't dare rinse it.

She nods at the kitchen table and smiles. I nod at the kitchen table and smile back. She hands me a mug of steaming black tea and pushes me towards the table. I finally remember the Kurdish for thank you, which sounds like *zor spas*. A flurry of plates appears. The honey is lighter than back home, the bread is darker. There is creamy goat's cheese and giant, juicy burgundy red grapes. She spoons fresh pomegranate seeds onto my plate from a large bowl. There is so much color. I take a tiny bite of cheese dipped in honey but it won't go down. Aunt Maya walks in as I start to cough and hands me a glass of water. She keeps her hand on my back as I drink, which makes drinking it even harder.

You meet Trahzia? Upon hearing her name, the woman washing dishes turns around and smiles. She is missing a side tooth.

I have, Aunt Maya.

Trahzia bring you anything what you want, Aunt Maya reassures.

Holding my breath, I meet Aunt Maya's gaze. My right eye twitches.

Today we go to shopping, Aunt Maya strokes my hair, and getting you ready for the school. Later we ride a – and

ALEX POPPE

here she makes a loop-de-loop motion with her hand – sound good? You shower and we go to the Family Land.

*

Do you want to know how I do it? How I keep my ache silent? How I can go shopping or ride roller coasters while Mom is in a sunless box under brown earth and Dad is blowing across the desert? Thinking about it starts The Pit of Loneliness twisting inside my gut and makes me want to stay under the hot shower until every bit of me melts down the drain.

Aunt Maya sits down so close I see the tiny hairs standing up on her neck. You talk about it Shatu?

No thanks.

Talking help, no? Aunt Maya asks.

No. No. It doesn't.

Aunt Maya has two sons, but they go to school in the UK. She started painting when the younger went abroad. Aunt Maya's paintings are like nothing I've seen in Nashville. She re-creates moments in Kurdish history on series of old wooden doors set in manufactured pathways of broken glass and rubble. She laughs without smiling when she tells me of breaking sheets of new glass and slabs of stone to make fake destroyed villages. Aunt Maya shows me some pictures of an installation she did for a museum in Halabja. The painted people look really creepy. Lots of melting noses, huge lifeless eyes, wide-open screaming mouths. Sometimes she attaches found objects so the paintings become like sculptures. There is one door with a charred stuffed animal dangling from a painted little girl's burnt hand. Aunt Maya's studio is housed in a cultural center that sometimes shows her work. She says the people

GIRL, WORLD

who should see her work don't go to cultural centers.

Saturday morning she goes to her studio so I'm left alone with Trahzia. By noon, I have unpacked my suitcases and filled the empty hangers in my closet. The starched white school uniform shirts look like they belong to someone else. Restless, I head to the library.

Ignoring the uh-oh feeling, I sit at Aunt Maya's desk and pull open a drawer that looks promising. Inside are wrinkled newspaper clippings detailing Uncle Mazen's death in 2004 when suicide bombers blew up the Kurdistan Democratic Party office and the Patriotic Union of Kurdistan office at the same time. Uncle Mazen was Aunt Maya's husband. Mom didn't come back for the funeral which was right after Dad's. For the first time I wonder if she regretted it. There is a Kurdish flag wrapped around a military medal and a silver-framed, old-fashioned photograph of Uncle Mazen with the current Kurdish President standing close to a young woman who looks an awful lot like Aunt Maya. I feel like a kid with her hand in the cookie jar when Trahzia comes in to dust.

She leans over me putting everything back into the drawer and gurgles something in singsong Kurdish. Then she pulls me up by the arm and leads me through the first floor to the part of the house where she lives with the driver. The insides of their rooms pulse with color. A massive orange and pink kiln dominates their sitting room. Cushions of every size and shade of red are thrown helter skelter around a low copper table. Green plants snake along the walls. There is so much life in the peaceful stillness of the space.

Trahzia seats me on a cushion near the window and lays my head back. She passes her hands over my eyes to close them. They smell like vanilla cake batter. Suddenly, something vibrates along my eyebrows. It sounds like a

ALEX POPPE

fingernail running along plastic comb teeth. I cock one eye open and watch two threads crisscross along my brow bone and disappear between Trahzia's teeth. A bead of saliva threatens the corner of her mouth.

She surveys her work with satisfaction and hands me a mirror. For a moment I don't recognize myself. The eyes that peer back at me seem bigger and somehow brighter. They look like Mom's eyes.

The sun glints off the mirror creating a spotlight and that's when I see it behind one of the winding vines. A photo of three young girls, two with red hair, dressed in traditional clothing, performing a dance. The third girl is missing a side tooth. My face pivots towards the photograph. Chopy, says Trahzia pointing at the picture. Chopy, says Trahzia as she takes my hand and pulls me up. Chopy, says Trahzia as she bounces from left foot to right foot travelling across the floor. I stand like a statue. I have never seen this dance.

Trahzia is determined to teach me the chopy steps. Left foot out. Were Mom and Trahzia and Aunt Maya all friends when they were kids? Right foot out. Why does Trahzia work for Aunt Maya? Cross left. Were they part of a dance troupe? Step right. Why is the President in an old picture with Mom? Left back. Where was Dad during all this? Left foot out. Are there more photos?

I point to the photograph and ask Trahzia for more. She starts to dance again. I shake my head no and point to the picture again. Trahzia lifts her shoulders. I mime taking a picture and she disappears behind a closed door. My body tightens and wants to throw itself among the crimson cushions, kicking and screaming. Trahzia returns holding a worn brown leather book.

The inside pages smell of cedar. The beginning photos

GIRL, WORLD

are all of Mom, Aunt Maya, and Trahzia when they were young. Here they are picnicking with family outside an ancient monastery carved into a hillside. Here they are in their dancing costumes at a family wedding by a lake. Here they are in school uniforms, Trahzia mugging for the camera, Mom wearing a hijab.

Trahzia wordlessly stops my hand from turning the page and looks at me with such seriousness that I am back in our kitchen in Nashville about to find out that Mom will never again make me macaroni and cheese with bread crumbs on top because she is never coming home. A sweat bead trickles down my armpit. The next page shows photos of homemade tents set against a backdrop of snow-capped mountains. There are too many people for the number of tents, all looking hungry and tired. A red-haired, dirty-faced teenager stares murderously while her hijabbed sister sits with her chin sunk onto her chest. Looking at the photos makes me feel like I'm lying under a slab of lead and maybe it would be better never to get up.

I stare at the hardened eyes captured in the photograph of Mom's face. My mom – my cartoon-voice-inventing, bed-sheet-fort-on-a-school-night-making, Meals-on-Wheels-delivering, Kurdish-immigrant, dead-from-a-hit-and-run-driver-fleeing-a-bomb-explosion-outside-a-mosque mom – looks like she could kill someone. Looking at Mom's eyes in that picture sends all my blood to my toes.

Anfal, Trahzia says, and goes catatonic. Then she shakes herself like a dog after a jump in a pond, snaps the album shut, and puts it somewhere only snooping will find.

Anfal?

I know about Anfal. Every Kurd knows at least the Wikipedia minimum. I didn't know Mom had actually lived it.

ALEX POPPE

What else don't I know? Aunt Maya comes home at 5:37.
Aunt Maya, I say, you're right. Talking might help.
Aunt Maya smiles, takes off her hijab, and sits down at the kitchen table. She pats the seat next to her.
I don't sit down. How long were you in the camps? What happened to Mom in the camps? Why did she stop wearing the hijab? Why is there a picture of Mom with the President? Where was Dad during all this?
Aunt Maya's head and shoulders slump as she bunches the headscarf on the table into a crumpled ball. She looks like the last plastic doll left on a K-Mart shelf at Christmas time. For about thirty seconds we both listen to air.
Anfal. The word escapes her mouth more than she says it. She goes into the library and returns with one of the books that has her surname on it. She tells me Uncle Mazen wrote about the eighth and final phase of Anfal in the Barzan heartland where Saddam killed Kurdistan Democratic Party families and demolished countless villages. Inside there are more pictures of destroyed villages and makeshift mountain camps.
You and Mom and Trahzia are from a Barzan village?
Aunt Maya nods her head.
I wonder if I am related to the President.
Trahzia puts out platters of food which no one eats. The firm basmati rice of the biryani sits in perfect mounds, bits of chicken and plump sultana peeping out. Chunks of eggplant, zucchini, peppers, and potatoes wait patiently in rich ripe tomato sauce for spoons that never come. There are side salads of green, purple, and orange to fill out the table. At home we used to have one main dish and one salad that we would share.
Trahzia still won't let me help clear the table. Aunt Maya

GIRL, WORLD

asks, How much tell you your mom the camps?
Some, I lie.
Aunt Maya leads me out onto the patio where we sit next to each other on a cushiony wicker loveseat. It seems strange to sit on living room furniture outside. The sun looks like a giant butterscotch candy coating the sky. Aunt Maya and I stare at it and listen to the zhur-zhur-zhur of lawn sprinklers as we both wait for her to begin.
There was whispers of marching and killing men. Our men going to mountains for training and fighting. Some men stay in village to protection. Saddam men come. We no see our men again. Saddam men do bad things. We womans running to mountains. Many Kurdish peoples running to mountains.
Aunt Maya is breathing heavily and stops speaking for many moments. A chorus of insects fills the silence followed by the bleating call to prayer. Nearby, someone is grilling chicken shish.
Your mom very beautiful, is what she says next.
Was Aunt Maya. Yes she was. My voice is so quiet I wonder if she hears me.
Bad mans doing bad thing to beautiful womans.
An olive green lizard darts across the marble-y stone and melds into the drab, dry grass.
Woman losing honor. Family losing honor. Important village man don't married woman haven't honor. Woman must to marry or… or, or must to…be no more for family having honor. Elders…say…in camp…mom no more for bringing back family honor. Your father hear and he steal her to America.
I remember the picture I found in Aunt Maya's desk. Did Mom and Dad love each other?

ALEX POPPE

There different kind of love. Your father loving Dilin since they small. Your mom grateful he marry to her and safe her. She loving him later.
Life has long, Aunt Maya says as she tries to put her arm around me.
I am not a hugger.

※

All night the thought's tentacles nip at the collar of my T-shirt, pin me in place, and choke me. If it happens eventually, why not do it now? Then at least The Pit of Loneliness wouldn't take root inside my stomach and hollow me from inside out. Mom and I could be together. I have already lost the smell of her. Annie spends the night on my pillow instead of on her shelf.
Trahzia, Aunt Maya says, joined the Peshmerga after her father and brothers were tortured and killed by the Ba'ath party in an underground prison. She fought with the Barzani tribe for the Kurdistan Democratic Party against Saddam during Anfal and against the Barzani tribe in the mid 1990's when the Barzanis teamed up with Saddam against the Patriotic Union of Kurdistan. It's hard to picture those same hands which fold flaky filo dough around nuts and honey holding one of those funny-looking rifles Aunt Maya's driver keeps in the car.
Now that Saddam is dead, Trahzia is no longer a soldier. Instead, she seems happy to wield a knife against a pile of multi-colored fruit or stuff rice and meat into vegetables. Sometimes I watch and we trade words as she cooks. She points to something she's chopping like a fig and says *hajir*. I point back and say fig. Then she usually gives me a piece.

GIRL, WORLD

I say *hajir* over and over again inside my head until I have swallowed. I don't know what she says inside her head as she chews. Sometimes she just stands real still and closes her eyes.

❋

I have been in Kurdistan for nine days when Lila calls me on Skype. Lila is a drummer in a surf rockabilly band and can't sleep with anything covering her feet. She lives across the hall from our old apartment in Nashville and used to babysit me when I was a little kid. It's 2:57 back home. Lila must have just finished a gig because her makeup looks runny. She asks how I'm doing. Hearing her gravelly southern twang cocoons me in Nashville hominess: the soft worn of a grandmother-crocheted Afghan blanket covering your shoulders, honky-tonk music drifting up from hidden courtyards, fireflies illuminating birch leaves, streetlights lending playing children an extra hour. And somehow in that buttered-toast scent of normal life, Lila sits at her laptop computer with a hand-rolled cigarette burning at her side to ask an orphan in Kurdistan how she is doing.

Lila sees my tight-line smile on her computer screen and tells me to breathe.

I ask her if she had a gig.

She says she did. It was a benefit for Mom and she wants to know which charity to send the money to in Mom's name. She knows the mosque needs money to rebuild. Do I want to send it there? Thinking about what happened to Mom in the camps makes me tell her to send it to Meals on Wheels and that I have to go.

She says she misses me. A new family has moved into

ALEX POPPE

our apartment and it just isn't the same. She takes a drag on her cigarette and blows me a smoke ring kiss, and with my one keystroke she is gone.

Some other mother and daughter are going to sit on our peanut curry spotted sofa cushions to play checkers. They are going to make Aqua Fresh toothpaste mustaches sharing one sink in our black and white bathroom. They'll drink honey ginger tea from the footed teacups Mom bought at a yard sale. They'll swing our old pillows that leak feathers in epic pillow fights on Sunday mornings. They'll use everything, all of our junk, and their spirits will push out our ghosts and someday not even Lila will miss us. And I'm living in luxury, and I've got all these memories but not the person who made them. I am seven thousand miles and five weeks away and every minute is a moment without the one person who made the world make sense. And I'm supposed to live with Aunt Maya in Kurdistan for like what, the rest of my life?

Thinking about some other mom helping her daughter with math homework at our wobbly kitchen table wakes the Pit of Loneliness inside my chest. The Pit stretches, its spiky circular blades whirling away my insides so all that is left is an empty husk. Falling back on my bed, the sound of the ocean rushes into my ears and I am drowning in muddy gray murkiness. I sink past Dad in his marine greens holding a bouquet of flowers in one hand and a 120 count Crayola Crayon box in the other. I sink past Mom smothering slices of green apple in chunky peanut butter as she devours *Entertainment Weekly*. I sink past Boo Radley tip toeing across a lawn to leave small presents in the hollow of a tree before running home and slamming his wooden trap door tightly shut.

GIRL, WORLD

The smell of baking cookies steals under my bedroom door. I smell the neighbor's sun-scorched freshly cut grass, and the desert's far-flung roasted sand, and the sharp animal scent of grazing sheep. Multi-colored pinpoints rain beneath my eyelids. Trahzia enters my room. Scents of cinnamon, cardamom, and coffee saunter in behind her. A drop of water slides down my cheek. She says something in swishy-slushy Kurdish and pulls me from the bed to the window which she closes. A fog of milky dust whips from the sky over the marble-y tiles and lawn.

Shamal, Trahzia says with admiration.

I don't know if shamal means dust or sand or wind, but whatever it is, it is pretty cool. It has power and awe and I want to swallow it whole into the Pit of Loneliness. I picture the shamal breaking the Pit's huge mechanical jaw hinges, grinding the Pit to a halt. As Trahzia and I wordlessly watch the storm bend and break young sapling trees and menace our window panes, and my insides slowly fill back in – I swear – an old man in a long white robe walks out of the center of the storm. The man has a white flowing beard and porcelain white bare feet and he carries what looks like prayer beads and he rights the broken-back trees and turns and roars at the storm. Then he gets absorbed into its center and disappears.

The wind completely dies just as suddenly as it started. Trahzia opens the window. The air smells sweet like cucumbers. The streets are absolutely silent. The trees have healed themselves upright.

Did you see him? I know you saw him. Look at that tree, I say pointing to a now-healthy young sapling.

Trahzia whispers what sounds like Mar Yosip and continues from room to room opening windows. I open Google.

ALEX POPPE

Aunt Maya gets home at 6:03.
Aunt Maya, I say. I want to go to church.

❋

Mom never talked about religion. The religion she grew up with said she was bad because someone did something bad to her even though she was following the rules. That doesn't seem fair. Aunt Maya says it's about culture too. Honor and purity are part of both Islam and being Kurdish, and I shouldn't turn my back on either, and would I like to try the hijab? The look on my face stops her argument mid-sentence. In the end, she buys me a modest long-sleeved navy blue dress with a round collar and sends me to the nearby Christian city of Ankawa with the driver.

The Christians in Ankawa are mostly Assyrian if you don't count the expats. Mar Yosip is the official saint of the Assyrian Church and is known for his gifts of mysticism and healing. Figuring a saint wouldn't seek the limelight, I head to Saint George's Assyrian Church because it is small and cozy. Aunt Maya says Mar Yosip is a long dead archbishop, not a saint that appears during sandstorms to repair broken trees and I shouldn't expect to find him in a pew praying. I point out that Trahzia said his name so she must have seen him too. Aunt Maya scowls at this and reminds me that lots of people refer to Santa Claus, but that doesn't mean he slides down their chimneys. This makes me smile because I don't expect Aunt Maya in her diamante hijab to argue a point using Santa Claus.

I am surprised when a round-bellied guard stops me at the church courtyard entrance to ask if I am a Christian. I lie uncertainly, causing him to half-heartedly search my

GIRL, WORLD

bag. I wonder who is watching us. Gravel paths snake around the vast courtyard behind guard posts and plots of needle-y grass before leading to the church's unadorned entrance.

The church seems much smaller from inside. Men sit on one side while women sit on the other. Most of the older women wear lace cloths on top of their heads. Some of the lace head coverings match one another like high school team jackets. The service is in Assyrian, so I understand nothing. There is chanting and incense burning and a procession around the pews. The priest carries a gold-covered Bible which some of the men kiss and the women gently pat before blessing themselves. And then it is over.

I am the last person to leave the church. I kick gravel from the paths as I stomp over to the car. The guard eyeballs me. I saw Mar Yosip. I saw him mend trees. I saw him quiet the storm. But inside his church, I felt nothing. No wonder Aunt Maya doesn't believe me. But if I didn't see Mar Yosip heal trees and calm a storm, how can I ever hope to fill the Pit of Loneliness? Its wrecking jaws scrape to life as I approach the car. I slam my car door startling the driver. The raw ache that is my insides swells until I am doubled over on the back seat. It is several minutes before I realize we are headed in the opposite direction of Aunt Maya's house.

Driving west past the airport, there is nothing but vast, empty land. We wind silently through the rugged reddish-brown foothills of Saffine Mountain until the driver pulls onto a chalky brown shoulder halfway hidden in a sun shadow. I hear a crescendoing popping noise that reminds me of exploding popcorn cooked old school in a pot over a stove top. As I lift my head Trahzia swaggers out from behind a small scab-colored ridge swinging one of those

ALEX POPPE

funny looking rifles over her shoulders and carrying homemade target boards in her hand. She moves like a gazelle towards the Land Rover.

She stashes her rifle in the back seat with me and slides into the front seat next to the driver and his rifle. Her rifle barrel is hot. She smiles a full smile as my fingers recoil from the gun's surface and then go back to cop a second feel. Breezy bouncy Kurdish volleys back and forth as the driver turns the car around and heads back to Aunt Maya's. It is the first time I have heard the driver's voice. It is smothered, like he doesn't want anyone to hear him. Trahzia's swings as she speaks. All of her radiates vitality. She must have an entire other life outside Aunt Maya's kitchen.

As soon as we get home I head straight to my room, take off all my clothes, and stand in front of the full length mirror in my cotton underwear. There is nothing gazelle like about me. Soft love handles droop over the elastic waist band of my bikini briefs. There is no space between my thighs when I stand with my feet together. Mom was pretty tall and Levi's thin. Then I sit down at my desk in front of a magnifying mirror. Annie is perched on the shelf above me. She watches as I study my face looking for traces of Mom. At certain angles I catch fleeting glimpses of her, and then she is gone, and I am left with my crowded reflection. My features seem too large for just one face. Annie slides herself onto my hand, hogs the mirror, and proclaims herself *GOR-geous*. Then she looks me up and down like a high school homecoming queen and returns to her shelf, shaking her beak from side to side.

Despite the heat, I change into sweat pants and a long sleeved T-shirt, slip out the back door, cut across the marble-y stone patio, squeeze through some manicured bushes

GIRL, WORLD

and exit the sub-division. It is the first time I have gone anywhere in Kurdistan alone. Looking down at my covered arms and legs I realize just how much my life has changed since Mom died. My insides start to twist so I pump my arms and legs to counteract the gut-spiraling. By the time I reach the highway, I am drenched with sweat and choking on the smoky, dusty air. I chug across to the other side where a radio tower looms over dirty hills from its solitary perch. Hot, fat, saliva-y tears streak my chin as I push myself towards it. The Pit of Loneliness jacks to life as I hit the steep incline. Roaring, it opens it maniacal mouth as I gulp down air and propel myself up the hill.

At the top, the guard station in front of the tower is vacant. Beyond it, the land crests, then gives way to mustardy green fields lazing in the distance. A few straggler sheep graze downhill. I wonder where their flock mates have gone. My run putters to a walk as the tears subside and my left hand uncups a mouth that I don't remember covering. The Pit grates to a halt as my breathing slows and deepens. Suddenly, the sheep lift their heads as if responding to some unheard signal and obediently trot over the next ridge. I follow, scurrying through overgrown brittle brush that smells like sewer water.

Clearing the top of the next hill, I glimpse the trailing hem of a white robe rounding a bend. Tips of long, white hair float behind it. I sprint towards the apparition encouraged by a chorus of contented bleating. Around the other side, the yellow green field has molted pearl gray puffs. Hundreds of sheep feed off the hillside. A young shepherd boy leaning on a wooden stick stares at me. I am suddenly grateful for sweatpants and long sleeves. A sugary breeze kicks up tickling under my chin. High atop

ALEX POPPE

a craggy cliff, the sun glints off something white, waving.

*

Every day I run over hills kicking up chalky dirt and avoiding camel spiders. Pushups and sit-ups follow. When I feel like quitting, I picture the confidence in Trahzia's jaunty stride when she carries her rifle. I think about Mom having to hide in mountain caves and later sneak out of Kurdistan on foot. In the shadow of early evening with bats circling the street lights, I outrun thoughts about what happened to her in between.

Aunt Maya's Anfal door panel series is being exhibited in Sami Abdulrahman Park. The exhibition is part of a "Reconciliation and Remembrance" conference featuring symposiums with international artists and humanitarian aid workers, and a field trip to Sulaimaniya to the Red Security Museum. Aunt Maya is one of the guest speakers so Trahzia and I get to go. The conference is held in the ballroom of the slick, shiny-polished Rotana Hotel and everyone who attends seems super-important. Trahzia and I sit next to each other on hard red velvet cushioned seats wearing oversized headphones attached to radio packs like the ones you get on museum tours. We tune into different channels for our respective languages, and when I get bored, I surf between Kurdish, Arabic, and English to see what I understand. There are mostly women in attendance, and the heady mix of perfume combined with the ripe smell of cigarette smoke from the corridor reminds me of going to one of Lila's gigs with Mom. Those days seem like a lifetime ago.

Aunt Maya takes the stage at 10:14 in a Calvin Klein suit and a hijab. It's like watching a badly dubbed movie

GIRL, WORLD

because I see her speak but hear a male voice translating in my headset. Of course she speaks in Kurdish; I don't know why I was expecting English. I am dumbfounded when she talks about the importance of honor, tradition, and forgiveness in maintaining the fabric of Kurdish society. My mind flashes to the mountain refugee camp photographs in Trahzia's album. I don't realize I am shaking my head from side to side until Trahzia pats my hand. Her cool palms are smooth like rice paper. They don't match the bright coral of her nails. This is the first time I have seen her wear nail polish.

    I wonder what Trahzia is thinking as we pile into a chartered bus and head for Sulaimaniya. She fought for the Barzani tribe during Anfal and against them during the Kurdish civil war. Does this give her a wiser perspective? She wears the same placid look that she has when she is chopping vegetables. I sit in the back so I can watch other people decide where and whom to sit with. Sometimes life seems like an extension of high school. Aunt Maya and the conference organizer sit together up front. We exchange smiles across a sea of covered and uncovered heads. The air smells vaguely of feet.

    The bus snakes southeast through pinky-red gorges dotted with small green bushes. Sometimes the hillside is lush and the bus has to wait for a herd of sheep to cross the road. Other times it is scraggy and barren like the wind has lashed it for the last ten thousand years. We stop at the Geli Ali Beg Waterfall to take pictures and cool our feet. Then we continue on a road that dips and rises like a rollercoaster so that my stomach meets my toes. Somewhere along the way I fall asleep and dream that I am the burnt little girl from Aunt Maya's door series but dressed in Scout's Halloween ham costume in *To Kill a Mockingbird*, and I'm trying to find my way home.

ALEX POPPE

The hills sprout trees as tall as radio towers strung with shiny silver prayer beads. All of the sudden a tree curtseys like a ballerina so I can climb on, then fully extends and passes me to a neighboring treetop. I treetop hop over meadows and deserts until I find a waterfall cascading into diamante crystals. I slide down into a cool pool that tastes like lemon ice.

The bus hits a sharp bump and jolts me awake. The inside of my mouth feels like hot cotton. Drool crusts the left side of my chin. Murmuring *bibure*, I lift my head from Trahzia's shoulder where it has imposed itself during my nap. She smiles at my awkward Kurdish word for sorry and hands me her bottle of water. The bus passes the manicured lawn of the American University of Sulaimania, Iraq before it arrives at the bullet pock-marked buildings surrounding the Red Security Museum, which is housed in one of Saddam's old torture facilities. There are dirt splattered tanks exhibited in the otherwise spartan courtyard. We enter through the Hall of Mirrors, which is decorated with 182,000 glass chards: one for each victim of Anfal, and 5,000 lights: one for each village wiped out by Saddam.

Inside the museum is a cold silence. There is almost no light. The air is thick and has no smell. There are torture rooms where men were stripped, hung up, and whipped into confessing. Remembering the long bumpy scars on the driver's back and shoulders, I look to see what Trahzia is doing, but she is not in this part of the exhibit. Next we enter the raping room, where female suspects or the wives of male suspects at large were tortured. It is actually two small rooms. One is a kind of holding area where women were left to wait, and the other is a smaller room where the attacks were committed. That way the women in the holding area could listen to what was in store for them.

GIRL, WORLD

Being in the raping room makes me feel like someone has stuffed me inside a burlap sack and pulled the drawstrings shut. I cross into the teen part of the prison and find a boy's crooked handwriting scrawled on a wall next to a bloody handprint. He is to be executed and claims that Saddam's men have forged his age so they can legally kill him. From the grave, he calls for someone to bear witness.

When I was nine, I got a wart on the middle section of my ring finger. When it became the size of an aspirin, I showed it to Mom. She took me down to the emergency room to have it burned out before it spread. The doctor tried to give me a shot of Novacane to numb my finger, but the needle was so big that I said no. Mom warned me that the burning was going to hurt worse than the shot and I should get it. Still I wouldn't give in. Mom tried to hold my other hand, but I wouldn't let her. I didn't close my eyes or look the other way. I watched as the wart was smoked off, charring my flesh, until my finger bled. Being in the Red Security Museum feels sort of like that.

I find Trahzia sitting on top of one of the tanks with a security guard. She is showing him his rifle. I smile at this and the burlap sack opens the teensiest bit. Even without a common language, I still know a lot about Trahzia. I know that she likes her weapons, be they kitchen knives or rifles. I know she is as loyal to Aunt Maya as she is to the driver, and I am pretty sure those two were on opposite sides during the Kurdish civil war. Trahzia seems to have found reconciliation with the violence that scorched these brown hills and robbed them of their trees. They say you never really know someone until you walk around in their shoes. Standing in the brown courtyard watching Aunt Maya pose with the guard and Trahzia, still holding his

ALEX POPPE

rifle, in front of the tank for a photo is a start.

*

    The tenth grade girls are drafted to perform a chopy dance at my school's Open House. I beg Aunt Maya to get me out of it, but she says no. I can't tell if it's because she's a stickler for rules or she's hoping this will be the start of my embracing Kurdish culture. In any case, as much as I practice with Trahzia, I just can't get it right. At rehearsal I hang out with Zerin and Glara, two other Kurdish-American girls. Zerin is from San Diego and Glara is from Texas. They both have moms. They can wear makeup and put their own pictures on their Facebook pages. They can't do the chopy. Whenever we crash into each other at practice, we have to say one thing we miss about back home.
    On Saturday morning at 9:59, the driver takes Aunt Maya, Trahzia, and me to the citadel. I need a traditional costume to perform the chopy in, and Aunt Maya can't be more excited. I am excited to see the citadel. People have lived there for over 6,000 years, which includes the Assyrian period of rule in Kurdistan. Maybe I'll find a book about Mar Yosip.
    At the citadel, I see very few foreigners. After we clamber up ancient broken steps and duck under stone arches, we head to the central square which surrounds a massive water fountain. In its cooling mists, women in abayas pose for pictures with their children. Some men are enjoying bulbed glasses of sugary black tea while smoking shisha pipes, which gurgle with every inhale. Try as I might, I can't imagine Mom in this place.
    Next we head to the fabric part of the bazaar. There is the constant smell of BO. The walkways are narrow and

GIRL, WORLD

throng with people. Some of them stare. Others whip out cell phones and take our picture. Some people recognize Aunt Maya and pressure us into their shops. I am amazed at how polite and smiley she is with all of them. Mom never had that kind of patience, especially in crowded malls. She would have been muttering under her breath.

Aunt Maya finally chooses a fabric shop. Inside there are too many options. Bolts upon bolts of brightly colored fabric vie for attention. I deliberately stare to blur my vision and let instinct guide me through the fuzzy choices towards a bolt of water-colored fabric with rhinestones. It is not until Aunt Maya hands the tailor a cloth-framed photograph of two young red-haired girls that I understand why I chose it. He points to Mom in the photo, then at me, and says *dayik*. My smile back to him is wavy. She was my mother; is she still? I agree to the same long dress thingy over floaty pants but draw a line at the hijab. Aunt Maya seems content with this. She one-arm hugs me around the shoulders. I let her and forget to look for a book on Mar Yosip.

The next week Trahzia and the driver take me to pick up my costume. We stop at a shwarma shop for something to eat. The place is teeming with families. Little children try not to spill on their shirt fronts while people pass napkins, hot sauce, and yoghurt cucumber topping from table to table. The smell of spices, grilled kifta, deep fried falafel, and too many bodies mingle together. The table tops are sticky. On the pickup counter lay a few stray fries. This is somewhere I can picture Mom eating but not Aunt Maya. I wonder if Trahzia was their glue. Someday I am going to learn enough Kurdish to ask her.

We arrive at the tailor's at 11:37. I change into my sea-swirl-blue costume. The running and the pushups and the

ALEX POPPE

sit-ups have had an effect. I look more like Mom and yet not. Trahzia loops her arm through mine and drags me to chopy in front of a full-length mirror. For a moment I can't tell if she is in the past or the present. The tailor watches for a while and says something in syncopated Kurdish. Trahzia meet his gaze in the mirror, nodding yes. The tailor comes closer and joins our chopy line. Looping his arm through mine, he says, You must to put your shoulders all in, and then he demonstrates. I try it. He is right. You must put all in.

Ras Al-Amud

One Friday evening, nineteen-year-old Yasmeen Al-Hashimy counts to 378 before a wave of contractions sends her squatting next to a green sofa back, hugging its worn edges for support. Time hovers. Her belly is gluey with sweat under her T-shirt and chador. Somewhere a neighbor is frying falafel. The smell of coriander and turmeric snakes through the living room causing Yasmeen's saliva to sour. Through the living room window, she sees the Holy City's fortress walls cut like jagged teeth against the sky. Behind them, the Dome of the Rock glows phosphorus. She considers waiting for her husband Ahmad to return from the mosque before leaving for the hospital, but the next contraction crescendos, pulling Yasmeen to the tile in its undertow.

One *As-salāmu alaykum*, two *As-salāmu alaykum*, three *As-salāmu alaykum*. She counts underneath the muezzin's *adhan*. She phones Ahmad. He must have silenced his mobile for the sunset call to prayer. She sends a text, grabs her identity card and pocketbook, and hauls her hopper-ball belly down the stairs to the roundabout by the Ras al-Amud Mosque hoping to glimpse Ahmad before hailing a shared taxi. The few cabs that are on the road are packed tight.

Yasmeen doubles over with the next contraction. A silver door handle glides into view. It is attached to a shiny black

ALEX POPPE

car that has stopped alongside her. A window rolls down. Over French pop music she hears an Islamic greeting and an invitation to get in. Levelling herself with the window, Yasmeen tastes the cool air inside the car. A single bead of sweat escapes from under her hijab. Her hands whisper over her head to make sure her headscarf is secure while the driver's gleaming fingernails alight on the steering wheel. Dismissing a pack of Gitanes cigarettes on the dashboard, Yasmeen lowers herself into the back seat and exhales the name of her hospital. The car smells of coconut and imitation Armani. She concentrates on breathing.

Beyond the roundabout, the sunbaked asphalt clogs with cars approaching the separation wall. Open-bed trucks carrying Palestinian grapes, olives, figs, and lemons from the Jordan Valley are stalled on the other side of the checkpoint where their fruit will spoil in the open heat in a few days' time. A ribbon of cars extends from both sides of the crossing towards the horizon.

Yasmeen's pelvis feels like it is separating. The pain flashes white and squeezes her. The back seat seems to twirl from left to right. What might be two minutes passes until the next contraction. Moments vanish during a breath. She pants in time to Nouvelle Vague's "In a Manner of Speaking" coming from the stereo.

'Lie back,' the driver suggests as he hands her an opened bottle of water. Hair gel separates his black curls. Yasmeen presses the bottle to her forehead. Cars slow to a crawl. Few horns dare protest this close to the Israel Defense Forces manning the checkpoint.

Yasmeen cries out with the next set of contractions. The car rolls two meters forward and stops. It vibrates beneath them. There are twenty-two cars between her and any one

GIRL, WORLD

of the four Israeli soldiers who should wave the car through to the access road that winds twenty-six kilometers around settlements and their security buffer zones to her hospital, which is twelve kilometers from her apartment. By the time the driver's car reaches the IDF guards, her contractions are ninety-two seconds apart and she longs for a toilet.

'Give me your identity cards within five seconds,' orders a soldier accompanied by a thirsty-looking German shepherd. Her voice shakes her words. When Yasmeen and the driver take more than five seconds, the soldier hands their cards back to them.

'Do it again. Five seconds. Mark. Go.' She takes a giant step backwards from the car. Her eyes flick to her right where the checkpoint commander, a man who looks capable of great violence, is smoking. The cherry on the commander's cigarette burns a brighter red with his inhalation.

'One, two, three, four, five.' An open hand extends just beyond the driver's reach. The soldier steps forward to snatch the cards from the driver's fingers, and then drops them through his open window when she hands them back. They land somewhere under the brake pedal. The driver's left jaw tendon spasms as his fingers stumble blindly along the carpet. His nostrils flare.

'Last chance.' She starts counting before the driver has picked them up. 'Onetwothreefourfive.' The numbers run together like a pack of stray dogs. 'Sixseveneightnineteneleventwelve.' When he finally hands them to her, she disappears with Yasmeen's and the driver's cards for three sets of contractions eighty-seven, eight-three, and seventy-nine seconds apart.

When the soldier returns, she hands them back their cards. 'Don't you see you're delaying the people behind

ALEX POPPE

you? You need to learn not to waste other people's time. End of the line.'

Before the driver can turn the car around, Yasmeen lets loose an animal sound and the smell of mulched vegetables fills the car's interior. Yasmeen's face rusts. The driver swings the car door open and places one foot on the graveled pavement. Throwing his cigarette to the ground, the commander points his M16 in the driver's direction and covers the space with two long strides. The barrel of his rifle comes level with the driver's nostrils. Time stretches.

'Why did you advance on my soldier?' He pushes the rifle a few inches closer to the driver's face. 'I could pull this trigger.' The driver has become a statue. His eyes resist the draw of the gun's barrel. 'Hands on top of your head.' Another gun covers Yasmeen and the driver as the commander pulls the driver from the car. He sees Yasmeen's watermelon belly. 'Fuck! Get her out of the car. Have the dog search it.' The commander cuffs the driver with zip ties and leaves him standing in the sun. The light is low, orange, and merciless. The commander turns off the ignition and stashes the keys on the car's roof.

Yasmeen's heart opens and closes very quickly inside her chest as the soldier grabs her under her arms and yanks her out of the backseat. Her chador is stained wet where she was sitting. Her water has broken and she smells feral. The German shepherd heads for Yasmeen's crotch. Yasmeen's blood swarms for a panicked moment until the soldier redirects the dog toward the car. Shadows lengthen as the sun skims the separation wall.

The dog finds nothing. Time skids. Approaching cars extend the stand-still line. The checkpoint is a wilderness of vehicles. An ambulance is called. The commander cuts

GIRL, WORLD

the zip ties, returns the car keys, and sends the car and its passengers to a waiting area off at the side. The driver turns his steering wheel as birds cross the sky like souls.

As he increases the distance between himself and the commander, fear creeps back down the driver's throat. A single blue vein throbs lengthwise bisecting his forehead. He needs to smoke. God is great. The pregnant woman's pungent water masked the Vaseline-encased marijuana bags hidden inside the backseat cushions.

He checks her progress in the rearview mirror. Where is her husband? He remembers how her hands settled her hijab before she climbed into the backseat, how her eyes darted to his cigarettes and faltered, how long she waited to lie back. She is not a dishonorable woman. What she has seen of life? Her eyes look young and old at the same time. What is her name? He knows better than to ask. In his line of work, exchanging names can break a person. 'I don't think your baby will wait for the ambulance.' His voice is like warm oil. 'I can take you to a friend. He's a doctor on this side of the checkpoint.'

Yasmeen's legs fight her modesty and spread. She croaks out a 'yes' and reaches for her mobile to call Ahmad now that the sky is the color of the sea. She concentrates on the pinpoints of oncoming headlights travelling between dirt splotches on the windshield.

Time ripples. Pain is a red-yellow flame licking at the edges of everything. The car stops. Someone drips cold water into her mouth and across her forehead. Ahmad's voice is in her ear. The smell of their fabric softener. Two sets of hands lift her from the car and carry her. The clap of hard-soled shoes on stone streets. Metal grates rattling shut. A child's shriek. Sounds braid. Up steps, around a corner, then

ALEX POPPE

straight. A hard turn. More steps. Cooler air blankets her. A sharp knock. Only once. A door opens. Shadows giving way to light. The harsh smell of antiseptic. New voices. They are hushed. A small prick in her arm. Someone takes her hand and brings it to his lips. Her fingers graze a five o'clock shadow: Ahmad. She freefalls into softness.

Beneath her are floating cushions. Voices come to her from the end of a long tunnel. She wraps her lips around the sounds she hears to decipher their secret code. Rummaging in her mind for a word, she understands that several voices are telling her to push. She feels the skin of not quite her upper thigh and not quite her pelvis flutter like a moth as it tears millimeter by millimeter. Pain glows outward in pulsating circles. Her insides are slippery fire. Her eyes focus on long square fingers that disappear between her legs. She feels them turn something inside her. The fingers belong to the hands of a man she has never seen before. A flash of panic. He pulls as he tells her to push. A shadow of a memory flits past her: there, then not. To her left she sees Ahmad's eyebrows knit into a caterpillar. His dark saucer eyes hold frozen tears. His lips round. *Push*. Muscles stretching. Ripping. *Push*. She pushes until what was inside her is outside her, and the Yasmeen that is left is no bigger than a girl.

The baby, a boy, has blue skin. He wears an umbilical cord necklace. The room hushes. He does not move. He does not cry. He does not make friends with life. Yasmeen and Ahmad never know the color of his eyes. Yasmeen's heart is suffocating. She turns her face away from her husband's tender head collapsed upon her bosom. His tears soak into her T-shirt, wetting the skin covering her breastbone. She does not stroke his head. She does not soothe him. Her

GIRL, WORLD

insides have been raked. A metallic bitter taste gloves her tongue. Yasmeen and Ahmad age years in the ferocious silence. As they limp from the doctor's house, darkness fades from a bloodshot sky.

❖

The earth rotates a tiny bit further. Back at their apartment, rooms shrink. Passing between the green sofa and TV, Yasmeen steps on Ahmad's foot. While he puts groceries away, Ahmad's elbow knocks Yasmeen's rib cage. Their mattress widens from the middle, leaving them on opposite edges of a tiny world. Words disintegrate across their bed and become the hum under a seashell.

The bedroom clock ticks. Ahmad reaches across the expanse of mattress for Yasmeen as she cocoons inward. There is a damp look on her face, grief or hate, it's hard to say. He wants to hold her close, smell the amber and honey of her soap on his skin. Something in his chest tightens.

Time slows; the walls fade away. She is lying above him, her soft charcoal eyes dancing, her waterfall of hair shielding them from everything. She traces his mouth with her thumb, sliding its padded tip over his lips to his whiskered chin. Her warm breath sprinkles baby names into his ear. He lingers in memory until his heart unfists itself.

The walls return; they feel tenuous. Under night's stillness, he listens to Yasmeen's measured breath in sleep, watches her face motionless except for its eyelids. Stroking a lock of her hair between his thumb and forefinger, Ahmad wills his wife to come back to herself. The woman beside him radiating intense heat as she slumbers is both Yasmeen and not.

More revolutions around the clock. Silence sets itself

ALEX POPPE

at the dinner table. Ahmad returns to his professorship, studying the past to understand the present. Yasmeen wants to erase the past, obliterate spirals of memory until there is nothing left but this moment beaded to the next. No shared history. No heart-breaking complexity. The loss of the son has drained all feeling for the father. Yasmeen is an empty Russian nesting doll, brittle and hollow. When Ahmad suggests they try again, she fills with bile.

Time zigzags. Two blue blankets with friendly yellow ducks, fourteen cloud-soft onesies, a garden of flower-embroidered hats, a tiny mountain of hand-knit booties. One large cocoa-colored bear as big as Yasmeen's sternum snuggles in her lap. Perched on the nursery floor, Yasmeen folds impossibly small T-shirts. She takes down the musical mobile of prismatic stars. She gathers bibs and burp cloths and hooded towels, and packs everything into a tidy garbage bag. The bear is the last to go. She lies back among the wasteland of her failed pregnancy and balances the bear on the soles of her feet. Her legs extend and stretch. One, two, three the bear is flying. On the underside of her eyelids a soundless movie plays: a boy crawling across tile to the green sofa, using it to pull himself up. That slow, wobbly first step forward. His candied breath warming her cheek with kisses. Tiny, trusting fingers wrapped around her wrist as they walk to his first day of school. Yasmeen's heart swells, pushing up into her throat. She cannot swallow. The film cuts. Her eyes open. The midday call to prayer wisps into the room as Yasmeen finishes packing.

❋

The old city is a maze of noise and fragrance. Two IDF

GIRL, WORLD

guards – one tall, one not – wearing ceramic bullet proof vests stand just inside the Damascus Gate, patrolling the main entrance to the Muslim Quarter. Raw sunlight beats down on Yasmeen's head as she twines through slivered streets to a charity shop. When she nears the Damascus Gate, her eyes lock on the soldiers' faces bronzed from the sun. Why are they laughing? The tall one's tiny square teeth do not match the architecture of his head. The small one spits over his right shoulder and laughs again. What right do they have to laugh? Yasmeen hugs the bag full of baby things to her chest while her thoughts flutter like caged butterflies. Tears heat the back of her throat. Her heartbeat thuds in her ears. In wondrous slowness, another version of herself rushes the guards and dumps the contents of the bag in front of their feet. *Look at what you did.* The teddy bear falls out first and lands backside up pointed towards the Western Wall. The butt of an M16 connects with Yasmeen's head. Everything dims.

Pictures flit back and forth and spin: the bear's decapitated head leaking stuffing, the musical mobile smashed into kaleidoscope glory, baby booties soaking up puddles of reddish brown water in front of a shawarma shop. When she lifts her head from the pavement, Yasmeen's skull pounds. Her shoulders tear at the sockets; her hands are zip-tied behind her back. Dust-filmed combat boots inch towards her belly. Her thoughts untangle. She is close enough to spit on those shoes if she dare.

'What were you thinking?' The tall soldier laces his fingers across his utility belt. His giant frame blocks the sun. 'You could have been shot. We didn't know what you had in that bag.'

Tick. Tick. Tick. Tick. Tick. Yasmeen says nothing. The not tall soldier watches from a distance. Yasmeen focuses

ALEX POPPE

on the bear's button eye and waits as patient as a stone. She feels the sun warm her face when the soldier squats down. Snip. Snip. Blood flows into her wrists and hands.

'Are you okay?'

Yasmeen's heart beats in confusion. A hard-faced woman in a faded chador picks up the duck blankets and stuffs them into a plastic bag. Somewhere a boy's throaty, high-pitched voice announces fig juice for sale. Yasmeen's gaze slides to the tall soldier. His face flows with concern. Doubt slips around her like eels.

'Can you stand?'

Yasmeen doesn't expect the soldier to extend his hand, nor does she expect to take it. Who knows which surprises her more? Something inside her loosens. Blood gallops to her head as she stands under the bowl of the sky. Its edges go dark and fuzzy. Her ankles are wobbly. She grasps his hand a moment longer. His palms are dry and smooth in the afternoon heat. He steadies her. 'Shukran,' she whispers before snatching her hand back.

The soldier smiles his tiny-toothed smile. 'Afwan.' And just like that, he lets Yasmeen go.

She wanders the labyrinth of shops as daylight unravels. Polygons of wild blue sky flow behind corrugated tin awnings. Yasmeen's eyes graze on mermaid-colored Roman glass snow-flaked with patina. The song of hawkers resounds down the lanes and resonates through her belly. Something too-long dormant and exquisitely fragile bubbles under her skin.

She sweeps from counter to counter as she samples dried apricots, fresh almonds, and agrarian basil. Anything with color. Anything with fragrance. Sweet cheese pastries taste like clouds; honey is a drizzle of thick sunlight rained to

GIRL, WORLD

earth. Next to Yasmeen, a Western woman in a sleeveless sundress, maybe American, orders baklava in accented Arabic. Her toned arms are golden; her uncovered head is sun-streaked. She wears no wedding band. On the black screen of her imagination, Yasmeen feels sunrays lap at her skin and warm her hair. She fills with a voluptuous panic. She envisions herself buying sweets in a foreign market, unencumbered, free.

The muezzin of the Al-Aqsa Mosque announces the sunset call to prayer, pulling Yasmeen from her reverie. To her right, a penguin of a woman in a black hijab negotiates a price for grape leaves. Their briny scent tickles Yasmeen's nostrils. Yasmeen imagines the woman's claw-like fingers mixing minced lamb meat with lemon scented rice for sarma stuffing. She sees the woman smooth a delicate grape leaf on top of her kitchen counter, spoon on the rice and meat concoction, fold neat, square corners into the sides of the leaf and roll, repeating the sequence until the bottom of her pan is covered in tight, green cigars.

To Yasmeen's left a young mother, who could be Yasmeen's twin, wrestles with her two-year-old son to seat him in his stroller. The son bellows, exercising the full force of his tiny lungs. He does not want to sit! He wants to explore. Yasmeen eyes the mother's belly, round with her second. Yasmeen's face empties. Something in her heart clicks shut: a captured infinite. Moments slip away under the muezzin's *iqama*. As the devout line up for the beginning of prayer, Yasmeen drifts home. The sun edges from the day.

❊

ALEX POPPE

Ahmad waits in the dark kitchen's silence. From somewhere come the muted sounds of dinnertime: muffled voices, clanking silver, sporadic laughter. His own table is bare.

The front door sighs open and coughs. The jangle of keys. Light footsteps murmur over the tile. The kitchen light snaps on. Ahmad blinks likes a caged animal in the harshness of its glare.

'Where were you?' His voice reverberates in the hushed room.

'In the old city.' The apartment reeks of sameness. Yasmeen starts washing green beans for *fasoulya khadra*. Water rumbles from the tap. A pot is set to boil.

'Yasmeen, what happened to all the baby things?' Ahmad's voice breaks.

Snap. Snap. Snap. Snap. Yasmeen halves the beans.

Ahmad's hands are on her shoulders. He turns her toward him. Yasmeen's eyes affix to the wall behind his left ear, to his slippered feet, to anywhere but his gaze. Ahmad takes her chin and tilts her face to his. He does not remove his hand. She concentrates on the follicles of dark hair just breaking the skin's surface above his upper lip. His face is shiny with the day's heat.

'What happened to the baby things?'

'I gave them away.' Yasmeen's voice is a fragmented susurration.

'What?'

'I gave them away in the old city.' She does not mention the bump on the back of her head nor the soldier who helped her stand.

'You had no right to do that.'

'I couldn't look at them anymore.'

'Yasmeen. We'll have a child. We'll have plenty of them.

GIRL, WORLD

We have our whole lives.'

Yasmeen backs up from Ahmad's embrace. She keeps her eyes focused on the acreage of his chest. 'I don't know.'

'What do you mean? It's our dream. Little ones of our own.'

'I don't know if it's my dream anymore.' The ensuing silence coats them.

Ahmad clears his throat. 'Since when?'

'Since that,' Yasmeen's breath skips, 'night.' Something inside her pulls taut.

Ahmad moves forward. Again his arms encircle her. Again she backs away. They two-step from the sink to the refrigerator. The water boils, rattling its pot on the burner.

'Habibti, you're grieving. We both are. I lost him too.' Ahmad's voice is a scratch beneath the floorboards. 'But I love you and I know you love me, and someday you'll want to try again.'

Yasmeen says nothing. She watches the scene as though observing actors in a stage play. The call to *Isha* prayer weaves through the kitchen. Ahmad's lips move in whispered recitation as he readies himself for the mosque. *There is no strength or power except from God.* Yasmeen wonders how much is faith, how much is habit, and how much is fear.

'I'm going to pray for guidance. You know your place is here with me.' His eyes are a limpid eternity. 'I love you Yasmeen.' The apartment door clicks shut.

Yasmeen resumes making dinner. She blanches the beans, turning them a lucent shade of green. The last bright thing inside her flickers. Outside her kitchen window, moonlight shatters against the Dome of the Rock. Inside her chest pulses something broken but unafraid.

The Crystal Fairies

Seraphina was born with the filigree pattern of a doily etched into her back. At six months it had not healed. When she was three and the Millers' big barking dog chased her, and she felt her feet leave the ground, she realized why it was there. Whenever she felt scared, iridescent, granite-colored wings emerged from the grooves in her skin. *You've got your head in the clouds*, her mother joked, and sometimes it was true.

The night before her first day of school, Seraphina's mother tried to steady her daughter's nerves, but Seraphina kept floating to the ceiling. Her mother shut all the windows before she doctored Seraphina's dresses. She cut back slits like gills so her wings could wave and edged the vents in pink trim and twinkling rhinestones. The televised Watergate Hearings played on the black and white in the corner. *How I wanted to fly when I was a girl,* her mother said as she sewed. Seraphina cur a stepstool and knew her wings were not the stuff of wishes.

Why did she have wings and her momma didn't? Standing side by side in front of the bathroom mirror, Seraphina's momma compared her dark green eyes to Seraphina's grass-colored ones, her chestnut coils to Seraphina's russet curls, the dimple in one chin to the smooth surface of the other. *Some things get passed down, and some things skip a generation or two.* Then her momma sat Seraphina on

GIRL, WORLD

the opaline stone vanity and told her about the Crystal Fairies, angels fallen into irredeemable love with mortals on earth. When the angels snuck down to woo their lovers, meteorites pummeled the earth. The man upstairs threw a mean fastball. If an angel made a wedding vow, God shut the pearly gates on him forever.

Sometimes Seraphina felt her skin splitting when she lay in bed. This was when the sensation was still new, when the wings scraped a little as they pushed through. In the dark and the alone of night with the Boogeyman panting in the closet, she had to turn on her stomach so her wings wouldn't get tangled in the sheets or rip the mattress. A little blood slid between the ridges of her rib cage and dribbled under her arms. But being airborne felt like floating in water and riding a Ferris wheel at the same time. Getting down was another story. Crash landings meant skinned elbows or bloody knees. To comfort her, Seraphina's momma said Seraphina might outgrow her wings when she got a smidgeon older and wasn't so afraid. Seraphina hung her head because she knew it wasn't true. She knew it when Michael Walker tried to kiss her after the eighth grade graduation dance and all he got was a mouthful of shoe.

With her back forever scabbed and deeply scarred by the time she was fifteen, Seraphina never swam at the quarry nor wore halters. At school she laughed off names of "Scaredy Bat" or "Bird Girl" and invitations to join a circus. She ignored the piles of chicken feathers left around her desk and the teeth-marked bread crusts heaped at her locker, and she didn't hold it against her classmates when they cornered her and tried to clip her wings. A few of them ended up with sore behinds when they fell off as she flew to safety, but no

ALEX POPPE

real harm was done. The art room's scissors were no match for her rock-skeletal wings. After that, she kept herself to herself and the other kids thought that was fine too. From beneath her thick fringe, she'd watch them cluster in the cafeteria, making plans for Saturday night, and she'd think about the Crystal Fairies.

Outside Heaven's gates, the banished Crystal Fairies cried big, salty tears but God remained resolute. Their tears collected space glitter and moon confetti. They grew fatter and thicker and heavier so when they fell to Earth, they crashed through the ground into the depths of the underworld. Pluto, who had no time for tears, set them on top of the highest mountains and let the rising Sierra Nevada do its trick. *We call it granite* Seraphina's mother said as she touched the shimmering walls of their house and then placed her hand on Seraphina's upper back. Their house had been built from the local pearly stone right before the railroad tracks were pulled up in the 1940's. And now those developers in their city suits were trying to take it as they had taken all the others during the twilight days of the town. But Seraphina's mother knew how to dig her heels in because she knew about the Crystal Fairies. How they followed their tears to the California valley when God wouldn't open his door. How they remained love-torn on earth, even as the land divided, even as it hibernated under ice. How the sculpting glaciers blended fairy bone with rock until the entire mountain range gleamed. *Nobody's going to force us from where we belong*, she said after the developers had finally gone. *This place is in our bones.* The salve she worked into Seraphina's skin felt both icy and hot at the same time. *See*, her momma'd say, pointing at Mount Whitney. And

GIRL, WORLD

the granite mountain glistened like crystal when the sun licked it, as if wetted by tears.

❋

Lucy Mae Whittlefield played Cupid in the Red Top Circus until her wings went ablaze after she stood too close to a fire twirler. She dyed her wings daily to keep them the aquamarine of her eyes. Richie Benson didn't sprout wings until his voice cracked and he grew facial hair. Things evolved in their own time; this was the point. Nature did as she pleased. And when people didn't understand Nature, they made up stories to explain her away. Seraphina had read about sirens and swan maidens and fallen angels, but she'd never met anyone like her in her thirty-seven years. How wondrous it would be to curl under someone's unfurled wing. To fly without fear.

Seraphina's house was her momma's house and her momma's before. With all her folk gone to the great beyond, Seraphina always left an upstairs window open, even in winter. A telephone extension cord stretched through it to the roof where she kept an old princess phone, a rope ladder, and an extra set of house keys. When she scared herself high like she had just done cleaning the gutters, she could always make her way down. Seraphina picked up the rope ladder from the roof top. It roughed her palms.

'Lady, how'd you get up there?' From the sidewalk below, a little girl blew a huge purple bubble from her wad of Hubba Bubba. She had her hand on her hip like a grown woman. 'I don't see no stairs.'

'I flew. Now I have to get down. Catch.' Seraphina threw her the other end of the rope ladder. Some things were easier to do knowing someone was waiting on the other side.

'What do I do with it?'

'Just hold it steady.'

Grabbing at the rope's tied off end, the girl plunked down to her knees. Her ribs poked through her T-shirt like the wires of a parakeet cage.

'Watch your head.' Seraphina hopped over the crouching girl.

'You want me to yank it down?'

'We'll leave it. How about an ice-cream reward? I hear the truck coming. You think your momma would mind?'

'She won't mind. Hey lady, are you hurt? There's blood on the back of your shirt. My momma always says you have to wash a cut. Then she gets this stingy stuff and puts it on and then she blows on it. I always tell her the blowing don't help none. When something stings, it stings.'

'You're right. When something stings, it stings.'

'And there's not a GD thing you can do about it.'

Seraphina hid a smile. 'Where do you live?'

'We live the next street over. We just moved in with my Uncle Ray, who's not really my uncle, but I'm not supposed to say that in public. I have to start Valley Middle School on Monday and I don't know what kind of kids these kids will be.'

Seraphina pulled on the back of her shirt to un-stick it from her open scabs. Blood slid into the waist band of her trousers. The little girl wore purple nail polish to match her gum. The left-hand nails were fairly neat, but the right-hand nails were a mess. Her toes fared somewhat better. 'Is purple your favorite color?'

'Way. I did them myself. They're good, huh? I can do yours if you want. Momma says she's gonna paint my room

GIRL, WORLD

any shade of purple I want when I turn eleven. That means I have to wait 'til October. That's just too long. I might die.' She clasped her hands in front of her chest like a heroine in a melodrama. Seraphina noticed the Hello Kitty ink stamps lining her forearm.

'I'm sure you'll work something out.'

'Yeah, probably. I'm pretty resourceful.'

'I have no doubt.' Seraphina pointed at the kitty-cat conga line stretching from the little girl's left elbow. 'What's that?'

'It's my stamp-on tattoo. I'm practicing for when I'm older. Momma says I can't get a real one till I'm sixteen and that's final!' The left side of her mouth snarled up to meet her nose and then settled back down. Now that Seraphina was closer, she could see the girl's lazy eye barely turning inward. She saw crusts of pink lipstick in the corners of her mouth, and a tear worrying the collar of her shirt. 'Lady, you ready for that ice-cream?' She slipped her warm hand into Seraphina's cold one and knocked her head on Seraphina's shoulder as they walked towards the ice-cream truck. 'I can never choose between chocolate and vanilla.' Her bottom lip thrust out with indecision. 'It doesn't seem right to take one and leave the other.' She lifted Seraphina's arm and draped it around her bony frame. In all Seraphina's life, nothing had fit so perfectly.

Her name was Stella Riley. In early October, her room was painted Snugglepuss-Periwinkle, and every afternoon she'd walk past Seraphina's on her way home from school, head bent towards the ground. Her sandals click-clacked down the sidewalk long after the air began to nip. She almost never carried books. Seraphina paid her five dollars to paint her finger and toe nails and another five to read to her while they dried. She bought her *Little Women* and *The Adventures of Huckleberry Finn*, and Stella looked dubious while she read

ALEX POPPE

aloud. Seraphina watched Stella's preadolescent face and saw the woman she would become twinning underneath it, in the flare of her nostrils and the upward turn of her mouth.

Ten dollars for the literary-spa treatment and another ten to clean out Seraphina's closets when the dry cold came and reaching up for anything on the shelves made the skin on her back split. Her wings were stiffening as she aged. Soon they wouldn't retract all the way inside her, and there'd be no hiding them. Outside the wind rushed down from the mountains, tinseling the air.

Stella was digging in the closet. 'You sure got a lot of stuff in here.' She emerged with a fedora astride her head. 'It'll take forever to get it sorted.'

'That was my momma's.' Seraphina pointed at the hat. 'I'll give you ten extra if you get it done today. And keep the fedora. It suits you.' She'd just as soon give Stella the money, but her momma might not like that. Better to have Stella earn it and learn the value of things. That's how Seraphina would do if Stella were hers.

She sat in an armchair and let Stella rummage. Her lungs were being crushed as the space inside her body filled. Dr. Bauman warned she'd have to get pleural fluid taps soon enough and probably surgery to re-inflate her lungs. Or, she could try radiation. Even though it was more advanced than it used to be, it still killed off the good with the bad, as some things in life tend to. Only the specialist would know for sure, and new options were being tested every day, and all she needed was a bit of good luck, and in the meantime, she'd have to stay strong.

Seraphina put her feet up on the bed and watched this perfect miniature woman separate the Goodwill items from the keepsakes. Seraphina wanted to cocoon her. Sometimes,

GIRL, WORLD

Stella'd hold up a frilly little something to her stick frame and twirl in front of Seraphina's full-length mirror. She'd curtsey, half-smile with her chin down, then throw her face up and to the side, laughing for a million imagined admirers. When she looked in the mirror again, she seemed surprised to see a skinny eleven-year-old girl staring back at her. She'd take a second, longer look; then she'd fold what was in her hand because those ten dollars were ready for the taking and there was a second-hand, twelve speed bike ripe for the having.

*

'Uncle Ray says I'm nothing but trouble.' Stella pushed the purple frame of her glasses higher on her nose and continued spring cleaning the living room windows. Puberty had made her lankier. She was all arms and legs in her cut-off denim shorts and tank top, lattice-like against the glass. 'I heard him tell Momma maybe we should rethink our living situation. I don't wanna move again.' She rested her forehead against the window and turned only when she heard the sound of cloth tearing.

Nacreous wings protruded from beneath Seraphina's shirt, which had mostly torn away. Stella saw her leaking scars when she grabbed Seraphina's legs to pull her down to the hand-woven rug. She touched one wavering fingertip to a wing. 'Does it hurt much?' Stella traced the wing's veins. The wing was hot like the temperature of a body, brittle but smooth.

'Not much.' Seraphina's voice sounded like caked dirt on hot asphalt.

'Love you for being a liar.' Stella kept her hand on Seraphina's shoulder. Seraphina's wings beat a small breeze

ALEX POPPE

into the room. The air smelled wet and metallic. 'How come you have them and no one else does?'

Because most people don't believe in angels, Seraphina didn't know what to say about the Crystal Fairies. How some of them didn't take to earthly ways. How they grew resentful of their mortal lovers and soaked the earth with tears of regret. How those tears gathered in huge chambers below the earth's surface where they bubbled into ashy bitterness. When Earth purged herself of such acidic discontent, fairy lament flowed within the lava, tinging the hills with melancholy. Not a lot of people know that the Sierra Nevada mist is made of fairy tears.

Seraphina grabbed a blanket off the sofa and wrapped it around her torso. She missed her momma, who would've known what to say. The blanket rippled behind her head. 'You're momma's probably wondering where you are,' was what she came up with.

'Did your momma have them too?'

Seraphina shook her head.

'So they're from your daddy?'

Seraphina gazed at the granite foothills framed in the window. Her momma's kin had lived among the glacial polished rock as far back as memory went. Seraphina didn't remember a daddy. She thought about the fairies whose bones were embedded in Owens Valley and the fairies who'd survived the Ice Age by teaming up with the jinn. 'It runs in the family. Sometimes, these things skip a generation or two.'

'All that runs in my family is drunkenness.'

The air rushed out of Seraphina's lungs as a grating sound drowned Stella out. Seraphina felt two jagged slabs squeezing her insides together.

'What the GD's goin on?' Stella moved towards the door.

GIRL, WORLD

'My wings are going back in.' Seraphina struggled to breath.

Stella swiveled forwards and backwards not knowing what to do.

Seraphina held on to a glimmering wall for support as the blanket she was wearing settled down around her. She wanted to remove it before the blood stuck it to her, but she saw the fear on Stella's face and left it where it was. 'You'd best be going.'

Stella didn't need to be told twice.

In time, all beautiful things go away. Spring gave way to summer, and Lone Pine Peak glistered from within, turning each crystal nook into an inferno of light. The days turned dry and hot while the nights stayed dry but cool. Seraphina was as restless as the rock dust blowing through her windows even as the odd jobs piled up around her.

Stella would disappear for stretches. She'd take off on her bike in her short shorts and purple Chucks before Uncle Ray and her mom went to work, and she wouldn't come back until sundown. She'd wave at Seraphina's living room window as she rode by, fast. When it was scorching, she'd stop by for some lemonade and tell Seraphina how Matt Geiger's braces nicked her lips when he French kissed her at the lighted baseball field. How Rudy McGovern took her swimming at the quarry and pressed himself against her under the water and it made her feel scared and excited at the same time. Shadow lashes danced over her sunburnt cheeks. *Was it like that for you?*

Other times, Stella chattered about her tattoo fund, which was growing, and she was just waiting to turn sixteen, was waiting for her boobs to develop, and *what was taking them so GD long?* Still skin and bones, Stella didn't need a bra, but

ALEX POPPE

she wore one anyway *for encouragement*. She said it might be a blessing in disguise since Uncle Ray liked big boobs, but then she dried up when Seraphina asked her to explain.

When Stella started high school, Seraphina saw even less of her. That was the way with young people. Seraphina waited for Stella to pass by her window until the evening sunlight turned a mandarin color. Then she'd go inside to fix herself a cold plate and eat it standing over the kitchen sink. Most of it wound up in the trash.

Stella made the cheerleading squad at Valley High and was always at the top of the pyramid. She'd catapult off and somersault to standing. Seraphina saw photos in the local newspaper, which she cut out and scrapbooked. What was it like to fly through the air with ease? To be admired for doing so? Stella smiled her megawatt smile because she knew how to take a picture. How to cock her head just so and look like she had a delicious secret.

'They say it's my birthday,' Stella sang as she danced a little step through Seraphina's front door the day after her sixteenth birthday. The cake sitting on Seraphina's kitchen counter was now a day old and sagged under its homemade purple frosting.

'Look!' Stella pulled a bony shoulder through the stretched-out neck of her T-shirt. A purple phoenix loomed from beneath its cotton rim. 'I designed the wings myself.' Stella was half way through her second piece of cake when she told Seraphina about the part-time job she had gotten at the diner in town two weeks back. She stole a look at the kitchen clock and gulped down the rest of her cake. *The cheerleaders* were waiting on her, and *you know how it is* and then she was gone, the screen door banging behind her, Seraphina's gift for Stella still wearing its bow, waiting for her on the counter.

GIRL, WORLD

Stella ditched her twelve-speed for a Vespa, much as she ditched high school. After she quit altogether, she moved in with her Marine Corps boyfriend, who was all tattoos and muscle. Stella worked at the diner, but without her cheerleading friends inviting her places, she had time to pick up odd jobs again, saving now for her get-out-of-Dodge fund. She kept it hidden in a brown paper bag underneath the kitchen sink. *What's his is ours but what's mine is mine.* Stella talked about going to Vegas to make some fast money or heading to Hollywood and putting her wide smile to good use. Not seventeen yet, Stella was already hardening.

Seraphina looked for projects to give her because sooner or later Stella'd be gone. While Stella worked, Seraphina hoarded Stella's expressions in her memory as she supervised from her crutches. Her partially retracted wings weighed heavily on her candy-cane spine. Soon, her home looked as nice as it had when her momma was alive, sewing slits into Seraphina's dresses. Tipped backwards in time, Seraphina was the momma and Stella was her skinny little bit with an upwards smile. Standing in the kitchen, Seraphina brushed crumbs from Stella's cheek and looked into those dubious eyes. One that turned barely inward. That bravado face Seraphina had known for almost half of Stella's life. Under the rattle of the kitchen exhaust fan, Stella jerked away. Seraphina's wings fluttered and her feet lost the floor. In the silence on the underside of Seraphina's eyelids, they held each other close, their arms encircling all the way round.

Stella was working the breakfast shift when Rudy McGovern and the prom queen came in for a post dance fuel up. The rest of their gang, mostly the cheerleaders and jocks, followed. In a few months they'd all be heading to college, to war in Afghanistan, or to fracking jobs in North Dakota.

ALEX POPPE

They were leaving. Right after her shift, Stella headed home and counted the contents of her secret paper bag. Then she packed a duffle and counted again. At nightfall she rode over to Seraphina's where the rope ladder still hung from the roof and an upstairs window was always open.

When Seraphina hadn't seen Stella for a long spell, she put on her roomiest shirt and called a taxi to drive her past the diner. She reached inside her mama's old sewing tin where she kept her household money, and that's when she found Stella's note. *Sorry.* Outside, the taxi honked its horn. Inside, Seraphina's home rushed with silence.

Loneliness is an exacting mistress. With Mount Whitney standing guard, Seraphina lidded her eyes and spilt out the quantity of her heart. Her mother used to say when you really love someone, the love envelops you both. That way you have some leftovers when the sad times come. We all have measures of good and bad; loving in spite of them is faith. That's why God sent Phanuel down to Earth to offer the Crystal Fairies a second chance. If they renounced their earthly lives, they could re-enter the pearly gates. Thinking everybody was better off with his own kind, some of the fairies followed Phanuel, not daring to look back at the ones they left behind. Others stayed. Still in cahoots with the jinn, they masquerade as homeless people muttering your unknowable truths for a few coins, or bewitch young women as shameless Lotharios. Those with a talent for healing become shaman.

Everybody knows it's impossible to beat time. Seraphina heard her mother's voice as the wind kicked through the trees and the days passed in stillness. At night, every breath drew a beat of her wings that shredded her skin. She was forty-five and her wings didn't retract anymore. They had grown too

GIRL, WORLD

big and stiff for her accordion spine. Her scars burned. Sometimes Seraphina felt her mother rubbing salve onto her skin, soothing all the places that hurt. Flight was overtaking her more and more as her time came near. She spent most of the rest of it in a nest of cushions on her rooftop. *There's nothing to be afraid of baby girl.* Her mother's breathy words tickled her ears as Seraphina headed for the clouds.

Family Matter

I'm pretty sure I could kill someone if I had to. Fico says I'd pussy out, but he complains about ball-sag and he's only fifteen, so what does he know? I'll check his palms the next time I see him, which will be in about two minutes. He likes to raid our kitchen after school.

Three – two – one. That's Fico knocking on the kitchen patio door before he slides it open. He thinks the knock shows he has manners. He beelines for the cabinets and fishes out something his mom won't buy him. Today it's a can of Pringles. When he rips off the foil seal and smiles so that his vampire tooth shows, I know exactly what he looked like when he was four. Your child-self shows when you're doing something purely joyful. Fico's child-self shows when he's performing or about to eat something he shouldn't.

I've known him since he was nine and I was ten, and his mom started talking to my dad about pre-adolescent junk food consumption in the checkout line at Jewel. Her version of flirting. Fico was petting a box of Twinkies in our shopping cart and I was scratching my mosquito bites until they bled. Fico and I got to talking because we were both there. Turned out he lived three streets away. Not a lot has changed since then except now he's at the performing arts school and I'm at the regular high school which means I get out earlier than he does and have way more free time.

GIRL, WORLD

Fico's first name is Frank, but no one calls him that. My name is Nastasia, but I want everyone to call me Nastia like the girls on my dance squad do. My mom had a big girl crush on Nastassja Kinski, so that's where the name comes from. That's all I know about my mom. That, and she left. No stories. No pictures. I used to joke with Dad that he invented her but he'd get so quiet, I stopped. No one likes father sulking. Dad's heart is a cabinet of a thousand little drawers, each one stuffed shut and locked.

I wait for Fico to lick all the potato chip crumbs off his fingers before I take his hand, palm-up, in mine. He's close enough for me to smell his sour cream and onion breath.

'What are you doing?'

'Reading your palm.'

Fico focuses on my right eye. 'What are you really doing?'

He swears the one eye changes from gray to brown when I lie. 'Checking for callouses. I don't want you to have ball cancer.' The truth is I can't afford to lose Fico. He's the second most important person in my life.

'What do callouses have to do with it?'

'Maybe your balls are saggy because maybe you jerk off too much. Callouses are a giveaway.'

'That's an urban myth.'

'Maybe they don't sag at all. Maybe you have high standards combined with low self-esteem. Maybe you should let me check.' When Fico and I were kids, we used to practice kissing until a bee stung him on his bottom lip, turning it red and puffy.

'That's okay.' Fico's right hand checks how pooch-y his belly is before he heads back to the cabinets.

'Don't be such a pussy. C'mon. I'm being a generous friend here.'

ALEX POPPE

He pulls out a package of Oreos and starts unscrewing cookie tops.

'You can check my breast. Tit for sac.'

'Got milk?'

'Right here.' I Scarlett-Johansson-up my voice as I lower my gaze and thrust my chest forward. Fico spits crumbs as he laughs. Neither of us take my flat-as-a-board chest seriously. If Mom had big ones, at least I'd have hope. But it's not like I can ask. 'Hey Pops, was Mom a meal or a mouthful?'

Fico stacks three Oreo tops and shoves them in his mouth. After he swallows, each tooth is outlined in black, which makes his vampire fang stand out. 'Wanna watch music videos?' He "Single Ladies" it into the living room before I've put the milk away.

'Hands on your knees and make 'em say please. In five, six, seven, and eight.' We both drop into a low squat, stick our butts out, and thrust our hips back and forth twerking up a frenzy. We don't realize Dad's come home until he silences the TV. 'Well hello Father.' I greet him using my best English accent. 'Would you care to join our soiree?' I like pretending to be other people. 'I think you could,' pause for dramatic effect, 'drop it like it's hot.' I bounce down into a deep plié and pop my hips back, a physical exclamation point.

They come into this world who they are, and we have very little to do with it. That is one of Dad's favorite sayings. He's a research scientist who sometimes looks at me like he doesn't know what to make of me. That's usually a good time to ask for something. Not something big like Beyoncé concert tickets, but something small like a privilege. I'm saving the Beyoncé discussion for later. So much in this world is timing.

I pirouette over to him and bow. His shoes are freshly

GIRL, WORLD

shined. 'Can Fico stay for dinner?'

'I'm sorry Nastasia. Fico has to go home. His mom already called me.' I one-legged lunge into a dying *Black Swan* routine.

'She called you because she thinks you're cute Dr Tyler.' Fico has no shame. He smiles like a kid who's made a fantastic mess and knows it.

'She called because she wants you home for dinner Fico.'

Parents always stick together. 'I can't believe you "Nastasia" me, but you "Fico" Fico.'

Fico and I traipse back into the kitchen for a last minute Oreo raid. I stuff cookies into his jacket pockets as he sucker-punches me. This is how we say goodbye.

'I'm going to wash up.'

I must have the only father who says "wash up" when he heads to the toilet. I want to hand him a magazine.

'Would you mind getting dinner started?' He flips through the mail as he heads upstairs. He almost never single-tasks.

I pick up the phone. 'Pizza or Thai?'

Crossing to the kitchen and dumping the mail on the counter, Dad takes the phone from my hand and replaces it on the receiver. He is close enough for me to see an angry whitehead threatening the groove of skin above his left nostril. Then he puts both his hands on my shoulders as if he's going to hug me, but doesn't. Dad's a mental-hugger. Even when I was a kid and he'd read me bedtime stories, he always sat across from me near my feet, watching me between eyefuls of words. I never sat under his arm. 'Why don't you fire up a salad?' He ruffles my hair with one hand as he picks up the mail with the other.

'Da-ad. Hair.'

By the time he comes back down, I've got the table set, salad made, and have swapped Lorde's *Pure Heroine* for TED

ALEX POPPE

Talks. It's an old one with Chimamanda Ngozi Adichie about if literature and pop culture and the news depict a group of people as only one thing over and over again, that is what they become. But do *they* think they are that single story, that stereotype, or is it only the outsiders who think that? I'll have to ask Dad. He always says perception is reality.

I put the salad on the table. 'This pizza looks really good.'

Dad ignores my comment. I'm the kind of grouser that needs an audience. He rummages through the refrigerator and adds his standard hummus, goat cheese, and olives to the spread. I'm lucky. I bet Fico's Mom made something disgusting like meat loaf.

I wonder what my mom would have made. Would she have prepared home-cooked American suppers of chicken, potato, and vegetable or would she have covered some frozen fish sticks in Cheez Whiz and called it a meal? I don't even know how Mom and Dad met. Was their first date over Mediterranean tapas in some cozy wine bar drenched in whiskey-colored light? Maybe that's why he's devoted to chickpeas at every meal. Who kissed whom first? If I'm anything like her, I bet it was Mom.

Dad pours juice for me and vino for him. When his back is turned, I switch the glasses to see if he'll notice. His wine tastes like a Jolly Rancher candy.

'There's something I want to talk to you about.' He places some organic olive oil on the table and switches the glasses back without a missing a beat. 'Sometimes the way you play with your friends changes as you get older…Marie Fico wouldn't approve of that dance you two were doing today…Both cultural factors and biology influence arousal.'

Dad seldom gets tangled in tightropes of sentences. I give him my big eyes and wait.

GIRL, WORLD

He goes into lecture mode to recover himself. 'Biological factors involved in sexual arousal and response are crucial to understanding the intricacies and positive aspects of sexual experience.'

From entertaining to mind-numbing in a nanosecond, I have to interrupt. 'Is this your birds and the bees talk? It's ok. I know all about the positive aspects of sex. I've been enjoying them for years.'

He takes a long moment. 'That's not funny.'

'It's a little funny.'

He says nothing. He looks as though I've just shot his dog.

'Dad, I hear you smiling.'

'I would appreciate your practicing abstinence, but I'm a realistic man. I do, however, expect you to be smart and safe in your choices. You know you can come to me with any questions or fears.'

If he were someone else's father, I would ask him for hand job tips just to mess with him.

'Was it a confluence of culture and biology with you and Mom?'

'Nastasia, what is important is your well-being and happiness.'

'What would serve my well-being and happiness is some answers. How am I supposed to know who I am if I don't know whom I come from?' The extraordinary privacy of Dad's conjugal affair with my mother frustrates me. Even if he told me something, I wouldn't gain any insight. There's no one and nothing to counter or corroborate. I want to open the freezer and yell into it.

'You came to me as you are. During your life, you'll discover yourself.'

'I love how you champion self-discovery until I want to

ALEX POPPE

find something out.' I get up to see what's left of the Pringles. 'While I'm at it,' the cabinet slams shut, 'I also love your system of selective response.' I can't remember ever being this exasperated with him.

'Too many aren't good for you.' His voice is a murmur.

'I know. It's a public service. I'm saving Fico from himself.' I crunch a stack of eight Pringles as I part-and-parcel Dad's face: wide-set green eyes, sharp planes in an otherwise broad countenance, a pronounced curvature to his upper lip. Twirling a dark curl of hair around my finger, I slip a single chip onto my tongue, letting the salt dissolve before I smash it against the roof of my mouth, Pringle shards inflicting a million tiny scratches. Dad's sandy hair is straight and smooth. I shovel in another heap. My chewing is rhythmic and mechanical. Words from the non-limbic part of my brain form a coherent sentence that the limbic part of my brain instinctively knows: there is no physical trace of Dad in me.

Fico calls later that night. I take my phone into the closet to make sure Dad can't hear me, which is stupid because he can't hear anything when he's working in his home office.

'Have you ever noticed that I look nothing like my father?'

'Yes. Did you just realize?'

'Don't you think that's weird?'

'I think it's weird you just realized.'

'I've been preoccupied with your issues of ball sag and such. Also, he never hugs me.'

'Lots of fathers avoid physical contact with their daughters when they start developing although your breasties have yet to blossom.' Whatever contraband he is eating clacks against his teeth as he laughs.

'If you were here, I'd punch you.' I scratch the arch of

GIRL, WORLD

my left foot with the toenails on my right. 'Do you think I'm adopted?'

'Could be.'

'I was kidding. You don't really think I'm adopted, do you?'

'Why don't you ask him?'

'I'm asking you. Do you think I'm adopted?'

'I wasn't present at the yoo-hoo sex that spawned you, so I wouldn't know. Go to the source.' Fico crunches something in his mouth.

'He never tells me anything personal. I asked him one question about Mom and him at dinner, and he shut the funk up. Are you munching Life Savers?'

'A Blow Pop. If he won't tell you anything, find out for yourself.'

'What, like hire a detective?'

'Like snoop through his desk. Where does he keep important papers? You might find your birth certificate. My mom's emergency money is in a plastic baggie at the bottom of a bag of flour. Her good jewelry is stashed under her date panties, our social security–'

'Ugh. Ok I get it.' Marie Fico could lose at least thirty pounds. 'So you're saying you'd go through my dad's office?'

'Me? No…no. Your dad intimidates me. But you should.'

'You wanna come over tomorrow and stand guard?'

'Can't. Rehearsal. Let me know how it goes.'

'How do you know I'm going to do it? I haven't decided.'

'You'll do it. You're like a dog with a bone. Good luck.'

I've never gone through Dad's stuff before.

He knocks on the door as I emerge from the closet. 'How's Fico?'

'Did you have a chip implanted in my head? How do you know I was talking to Fico?' I settle on my bed and

146

ALEX POPPE

open my Kindle.

'I have something that might interest you.' His face is a blank egg.

He pulls a chair up to my bed and hands me a slim manila file folder. Between official looking forms and a birth certificate written in Cyrillic are mug-shot type photos of a young woman with dark curly hair like mine. I give the folder a huge smile. From her profile shots, I see we share the same strong nose, the same high forehead. The portrait shot is cropped at her clavicle. Figures.

'This is Danica Babic, your mother. Of Russian-Serbian descent. Orphaned during the collapse of the Soviet Union. Finished her secondary education in Kiev and received a full scholarship to the University of Iowa, where I met her.' Dad's voice is clinical, not the voice of a jilted lover. I don't expect tears, but I don't expect the Tin Man either. Maybe I'm the result of a drunken spray and pray.

My armpits start swamp-sweating. 'Those Russian-Serbian genes trumped your American ones.'

Dad says nothing.

I can't not pick a scab. 'I don't look like you *at all*.'

'You do, here and there.' He vaguely gestures towards his chin.

'It's like we're not even related.'

Dad looks constipated.

The thought hangs in the air like a silent fart. 'Am I adopted?'

Dad's features shuffle about his face and settle down askew. 'Yes.'

I stop breathing for a long moment. The walls go wavy. This conversation needs immediate euthanasia. Everything I thought I knew implodes in one syllable. 'I can't believe

GIRL, WORLD

you told me like that. Where are my emotional coddling and mental preparation?'

'You're ready.'

'I don't feel ready.' I feel small. I hope he can't hear the tears inside my voice. 'I can't believe I had to ask you. You should have told me first. Did you even know her?' No wonder he never shared any of their stories. They don't exist.

'Yes. I knew her throughout her pregnancy and your birth.'

'How did you meet her?'

'I told you. At the university.'

'But how? Was it some meet-cute or was she part of some kind of paid research?'

'She participated in a study.'

'Sex and checks make the world go round.' Outside, the Harrison's dog barks and barks. Dad and I listen together, isolated by our separate thoughts. 'Do you know who my father is?'

'I am your father.'

'You know what I mean.'

'I am your father.' The force with which he says this sentence surprises us both. Dad coughs. 'I know this is a lot to comprehend at once. Let's take a break for tonight.' My eyes stay glued to the folder as he tucks it back under his arm. It seems like Dad should stay to comfort me, so maybe he does. Except he doesn't. He pats my knee before he and the folder exit the bedroom.

My whole body feels shucked. Did that just really happen? I grab the phone and head into the closet.

Fico is watching *Glee*. 'What's up?'

'I am adopted.'

'What? No way.' He silences his TV.

ALEX POPPE

'Way.' In my head, I'm standing at the edge of a precipice.
'What'd he say?'
'He brought in pictures of this Russian-Serbian woman who is my mother. He said they had met at the university. He said_____.'
'What? I can't hear you.'
'You hear me. You're not listening. He said_____. You know, he left out a lot when he told me the truth.'
'That sucks. Now you have to snoop. You have a right to find out what he's not telling you.'
'The thing is, if he left it out, it's probably bad. I don't know if I wanna hear it.'
'No offense, but it can't get much worse.'
'Yes it can. What if my real dad is one of America's Most Wanted?'
'The statistical probability of that happening to two kids from the same junior high is null.'
'I want to find my mom. Damn. He took the folder with her info with him.'
'You have to snoop.'
'What if she has another daughter?'
'So? You'd get a sister.'
'Why didn't she keep me if she kept the other one?'
'She might not have wanted to have you. Or maybe she wasn't ready. Maybe she was in a bad place.'
'Ouch. So much for my desire to live like the *Gilmore Girls*.'
'I'm just saying. You need to be prepared. You also need to snoop to find out.'
'What if she's dead? I'll never find out anything.'
'You'll never find out if you don't snoop. Snoop!'

GIRL, WORLD

'Okay. Okay. Tomorrow. I wish you didn't have rehearsal. Call me when you get out.'

'Okay. Happy snooping.'

I am gutted. I climb into bed without brushing my teeth. Usually, I knock on Dad's office door and wait for him to open it before I say good night. Everything is different now the tether's been cut. I curl up next to the Zoe Muppet doll my so-called father gave me for my sixth birthday and cough silent, dry tears into the top of her head. Her green, plastic eyes are worn almost free of their color. Her heart-shaped tongue dominates her gaping red mouth. I settle her into the crook of my neck with my heart in my mouth too.

Morning comes just as I fall asleep. Outside a car alarm urges me from my bed. The day is five seconds old and already full of lead. Both Dad and breakfast are at the table by the time I get downstairs. Chick peas atop of hominy keep his coffee company. The spoon beside his grits gleams.

'Good morning Nastasia. Do you have everything you need for school?' Dad is a disembodied voice behind his *Wall Street Journal*.

If that's the way he's going to play it, fine. 'Good morning Father. Yes, I have packed my carryall quite well thank you.' I sound like a casting reject from *Harry Potter*. When I pull out my chair, he lowers his paper. There are maroon aprons under his eyes. 'Your eyes are puffy.'

'Yours too,' he counters.

A rare moment of reality.

'Nothing has changed. You are my daughter and I love you.' His paper pops back into place.

I knock at his newspaper. 'Hey Mr. Gorbachev. Tear down this wall.' He closes the paper and folds it. 'I want to find my mother.' I interrupt his inhalation. 'I want to find her.' We stare

ALEX POPPE

at each other eyes level, jaws set. Carbon copies in stance. Ha! He blinks first.

'I'll see what I can do.' He smiles. People can smile and still be villains. 'Let's go. We don't want to be late.' Dad stands up from the table: first his head, then his shoulders, next his chest and stomach, and finally his legs. He leaves in a series of pieces.

❊

Skipping dance squad rehearsal, I race home after school only to skid to a stop outside Dad's office door. The grandfather clock ticks the minutes away. Fico's "snoop" song worm burrows in my head. I watch my hand turn the door knob as though observing it in a rear view mirror. My cheeks lift into the type of smile people have when they're doing something unexpected.

It is just a room I have entered. It is just a desk drawer I have opened. It is just the key to the filing cabinet I have found at the bottom of a box of paperclips. To get peace of mind, I tell myself small lies about something big.

Goodbye desk, hello filing cabinet. Open, rummage, shut. Open rum–holy shit! One, no two entire drawers are dedicated to me. The files are organized by year, starting with my birth certificate (father: unknown) and ending with a record of how many Pringles I ate last night and my father's handwritten diagnosis of my mental state. *Subject's rebellious behavior concerning knowledge of her mother demonstrates an uncompromising desire to know more about her lineage. Her ability to control her anger and frustration bears witness to her maturity. Therefore, she was availed to certain facts concerning her biological origins. Her exhibition of anxiety*

GIRL, WORLD

and aggression concerning the subject of her paternity prevented her from being told the scope of the experiment and her participation in it. I read his notes again. A kernel of understanding takes a lap around my mind and slaps me with this realization: I am the experiment. But an experiment in what?

In my head, I've fallen off that huge precipice and am clinging to an outstretched hand.

Reading the files is like reading a quantitative textbook of my life. Weight and height measurements, records of first word, first tooth, first step, first period, first kiss (how'd he know?) eating habits, hobbies, participation in clubs, analyses of social interaction, talent assessments, vocabulary acquisition, reading levels, development of analytical and problem solving skills, academic and physical achievements, charted character development – it's all in the second and third drawers. Memories cartwheel out of my head and stack neatly into their respective files. They don't belong to me anymore. They were created to service a fiction. I feel as though I put cotton candy in my mouth but swallowed razor blades.

Dad opens the front door.

I'm sitting behind his desk with a small, metal garbage bin filled with the most important looking papers from the me – files at my feet. Cupped in my left hand is a book of matches. His office door is wide open.

Dad finds me in thirty-seven seconds. 'What are you doing in my office?'

'Nothing.' Sometimes I play dumb when it would be better to be dumb.

'Nastasia, I insist you apologize for violating my trust and leave my office. I don't want to start locking doors.'

'I violated *your* trust? "Her exhibition of anxiety and

ALEX POPPE

aggression concerning the subject of her paternity prevented her from being told the scope of the experiment and her participation in it." What about my trust? What is the experiment?'

'Where did you find that? I keep that cabinet locked.'

'And this key opens it.' A thin key ring hula-hoops around my right index finger. 'What is the experiment?'

'You had no right to go through my research.'

'This is true. But you had no right to make me your research. What is the experiment?'

For someone who regularly interrogates the world, Dad is uncharacteristically silent.

I place the metal bin on top of his desk. 'If you don't tell me, I will strike this match and burn these papers from my files. I'm not kidding.' Dad topples forward like a lightening-struck tree, but I don't care. Even my hard-to-reach places hurt. My arms cocoon the bin.

'Your mother was a surrogate participant in a research study combining gestational surgery and gene manipulation. An egg from Danica Babic was combined with a donor sperm that had been genetically manipulated by me to enhance physical grace, coordination, and skill; to maximize verbal capacity and facility with language; and to stimulate creativity. Six–'

'Wait. You messed with my DNA like some genetically modified guinea pig?'

'Genes were enhanced for the study. Six embryos were created.'

'Do I have brothers and sisters?'

Dad swallows hard. 'No.' He moves slightly forward.

I hug the bin tighter and move slightly back. 'Don't underestimate me.' My voice is low and controlled, concealing

GIRL, WORLD

my Viking anger. I need to get less human to finish this conversation. I shape-shift into an ice queen.

He takes a step back. 'At that point, the government pressured the research center to destroy the embryos. I couldn't do that. The embryos were the culmination of a decade of work. Danica agreed to continue the surrogacy in exchange for monetary compensation. Pre-implantation genetic diagnosis determined which four embryos were destroyed to satisfy the investigators and which two were transferred. When both were successfully implanted into the uterus, selective termination was employed to reduce the number of viable pregnancies to one.'

'So I had a brother or sister and you killed them. How did you decide which of us to keep?'

'One embryo was sacrificed to minimize complications for the other. Genetic profiling determined the fitter of the two.'

'Kind of like *The Hunger Games* for fetuses?'

'For practical purposes, Danica moved into this house so I could monitor both of you, and we maintained the semblance of a couple. Our contract concluded with your birth.'

My blood feels carbonated. The man across from me watches and waits. He is no doubt taking mental notes for his precious files. 'I'm Frankenstein's test tube baby.'

'You are my daughter.'

'Really? I don't know who you are.'

'I know it's a shock, but–'

'Dr Tyler, *don't*.' There is no way I can call this man before me "Dad". I lean my cheek against the garbage bin and exhale a long stale breath. There's a small fire in the back of my throat. In my head, that outstretched hand I've been clinging to lets go, and I free fall. The movie of my life trundles up from somewhere: my so-called father teaching

ALEX POPPE

me how to ride a bike, holding my hand snorkeling in the Pacific Ocean, taking me to the Goodman Theatre in Chicago. There were birthday parties and Christmas trees and ballet recitals. 'Was any of it real?' I empty the papers onto his desk and put the bin back on the floor. 'Or was it all just for this?'

'It was real. As soon as I saw you, I loved you, Daughter.' He has never called me that. Bold. 'You loved your research and wanted to finish it to become famous.'

'I wanted to love and nurture another human being.'

'Right. You're hollow where your heart should be. You never even hug me. You did it for ego.' The look on Dad's – Dr Tyler's – face makes me wish I had swallowed those words instead of spitting them out.

'That's fair. It started out as ego but changed. You were a perfect miniature of your mother. I couldn't have engineered that.' When he mentions Mom, his eyes are two bright lights.

'Did you love her?'

'As much as someone hollow of heart can. In my own way.'

'Did you ask her to stay?'

'Danica always had a plan of her own.'

'Why didn't she want me?'

'She never met you. She wouldn't look at you or touch you after delivery. I think giving you up was harder than she expected.'

'You don't have to make me feel better. I don't even believe you. Maybe all she saw when I crowned was your genetic mutation inside a meat costume.' This sucks. I hate him and I don't.

'Nastasia, I always intended on telling you. I didn't know how. I'm sorry.'

'I'm sorry should have been your first words. So now

GIRL, WORLD

what? I assume you'll write up some more notes on my "anxiety and aggression" concerning this series of revelations. But then? Were you planning on publishing this study?' The thought of everyone at school finding out makes my heart pinball inside my chest.

'I won't publish it until the political landscape changes.'
'You won't publish it ever.'
'Politics will eventually catch up to science.'
'You're not listening. You can't do that to me.'
'This study will change the future of gene therapy. It will be published with the strictest confidentiality.'
'Get real. People will know the subject is me.'
'It will appear in scientific publications only.'
'You can't guarantee that. Not in the internet age.'
'Think of how many generations this study could help.'
'I don't care. I want a normal life.'
'Nastasia, one day you'll thank me. Look how talented I made you. I've given you an extraordinary life.'

I want to slap that obsequious smile from his face. 'That remains to be seen.' I stand and clear my throat, adopting an adjudicatory tone. 'I want to find my mother. I expect your full cooperation and financial support.' I don't tell him I have already squirreled away anything important concerning Danica Babie. Like everything else, he probably already knows. 'Goodnight Dr Tyler.' I leave him surrounded by the paper fruits of his labor.

There are twelve missed phone calls and three text messages from Fico by the time I ensconce myself inside my bedroom closet. Anxiety rides up my spine. Fico's hello is a steady hand on my back.

'What happened?'
'I was created in a petri dish.'

ALEX POPPE

'What?'

'I'm almost human. Or enhanced human. Dr Tyler played God with my DNA and paid my mother for her chromosomal contribution. Then he rented her womb for nine months and kept copious notes about the undertaking, intended for publication.'

The silence that follows is larger than the closet. Oxygen molecules strobe by, but none enter my lungs. 'Are you still there?'

'Of course.' Fico's voice is the last true thing inside my world.

'PS, I have no idea who donated the original spermatozoon.'

'Let me get this straight. The Russian-Serbian lady is your mom. Your sperm donor dad is unknown. Your dad dad–'

'Ex-dad. I hate him.'

'You hate him now, but you won't hate him forever. Maybe he predicted a day such as this and enhanced your ability to forgive.' He laughs alone.

'Too soon.'

'Sorry. Your...what are you calling your ex-dad now?'

'Dr Tyler.'

'Okay. Dr Tyler enhanced your DNA. What does that mean?'

'He jacked it. I don't know. He souped up the sperm side of things, He made me better in language and physical stuff and creativity.'

'You are so gonna kill the SAT next year.'

'That's not the point. I'm just research to him. He's using me. He doesn't really care about me. He doesn't...,' my breathing gets shallow and my eyes sting.

'It's okay.'

'Doesn't love me.'

GIRL, WORLD

Fico hums a song that sounds like a pink sunset reflected on water. 'It's okay.'

'Thanks.' I'm glad Fico can't see me wipe my snot on my sleeve. 'And he wants to publish his findings, and then everyone will think I'm a freak. My life is over.'

'No it's not. You got extra of all the good stuff. In a way, you're really lucky.'

'That's what Dr Franken-Tyler said.'

'Well, it's true. Now I can stop resenting how great you are at everything, You were made that way."

Fico's smile is a multi-colored whorl over the 4G network. I wonder if the NSA hears it too. 'You can't tell anyone. Swear.'

'Swear. What are you going to do?'

'Find my mother. And then I don't know.'

'I'm here if you need me.'

'I know.' My words are choked. My eyelids are droopy. Fico and I hang up in silence.

The house is still when I exit the closet. Even with the bedroom door locked, an uneasiness wraps its bony fingers around my throat and tightens. I retrieve Danica's folder from underneath my shirt. Sweat from the small of my back has dampened it. The photographs inside roll at their edges. When these pictures were taken, she was four years older than I am now. She looks like she knows who she is. Most of the time I feel like I am watching myself from the corner of the ceiling, shaking my head at all the stupid stuff I say. She isn't the prettiest woman in the room, but she's the one you'd think about long after the party's over. Her eyes are an enigma. No wonder Dr Tyler was drawn to her. He could have spent the rest of his life puzzling them out if she had let him. I alternate staring at her photographs

ALEX POPPE

with Googling films about genetic mutation and learning the Cyrillic alphabet. By the time I snuggle next to Zoe, I can write both our names in Russian on the blackboard under my eyelids.

A nagging thought hooks my nightshirt and yanks me from sleep. Needing a resurrection potion, I stumble into the kitchen in search of a grande mochachino. Hating Dr Tyler has drained my energy.

He enters just as the milk is frothed. I bet he has hidden cameras in every room of the house. Dr Tyler is wearing his clothes from yesterday. I've never seen his boring handsomeness so disheveled. I give him my best mean-girl glare.

'Good morning.'

Zero points for originality, but then I am the one with the extra dose of creativity. 'Morning.' He crosses left towards the counter so I cross left to the table. The ballast of a fixed distance between us keeps the kitchen from toppling over.

'What would you have done if your genetically improvised recipe had produced a vegetable?' As soon as I blurt out the question, my shoulders sink down from my ears. The coffee cup in Dr Tyler's hand hangs suspended between the cabinet and the counter.

'Pre-implantation genetic diagnosis safeguarded against that.' He clacks the cup onto the counter.

'What if PIG diagnosis had missed something and you didn't realize I was dumb, clumsy, and untalented until I was three. Would an unfortunate accident have befallen me?'

If Franken-Tyler were capable of remorse, I would think those were tears in his eyes.

'Nastasia, do you think I am a monster?'

'A monster-maker.'

'You are not a monster.'

GIRL, WORLD

'According to a bad batch of Hollywood blockbusters, I am. Gene-mutant is my single story.'

'You will play many roles in your life: mother, wife, daughter. You're *my* daughter. A sperm donation doesn't determine that.'

'Technically it does. Anyway, would you have thrown out the baby with the bathwater if I weren't one half of the wunderkinder?'

'Of course not.'

'Ever wish you had kept the other one?'

'No.'

'Lucky coin toss.'

'No.'

'Good for us there's no way to know.'

He approaches the table. I counter towards the refrigerator. 'What if I were just an early bloomer? If I had turned out ordinary, would you have declared the experiment a failure and farmed me out to some old lady in the woods?'

'Nastasia, of course not. I created you. I watched you grow inside Danica's womb with anticipation. I named you. You belong here, with me.'

'Another lie. She named me. After Nastassja Kinski.'

'I named you. She signed the adoption papers and left.'

'Why should I believe you?'

'I'm telling you the truth.'

'Prove it. Help me find my mother.'

'Why?'

'I want to hear her side of things.'

'She's not going to tell you anything different.'

'Then you have no reason not to help me.' He can't be the only one who gets what he wants. I open the refrigerator, take out the container of hummus he'll want for

ALEX POPPE

breakfast, and dump it into the sink. 'My word, how some things spoil.' My drawl is as thick as a drunk preacher's. The *Wall Street Journal* thwacks against the front door as I head to the shower.

Dr Tyler and I become less three-dimensional so we can keep on living together. I drop dance squad because it doesn't seem fair to exploit my genetically manipulated competitive advantage. Plus, it messes up some of Franken-T's research. I know better than to ask him to stop, but that doesn't mean I have to be cooperative. While Fico rehearses, I learn Russian and trawl social media looking for my mother. In the evenings, Dr Tyler scurries to his office, no doubt recording his privileged observations. The house radiates the conviviality of an autopsy room.

Of the eleven Facebook entries for Danica Babic, eight lead nowhere. The other three have privacy settings set so high, they defeat the purpose of social media. I eliminate one of them through a cross reference on LinkedIn. The other LinkedIn profiles ax themselves with their photos. None of those Danica Babics resemble the Lady of the Manila Folder.

A Pinterest posting makes me cry out even though there is no one to hear me. The cover photo of one Danica Babic in Serbia shows a tightly-framed nose parting two curtains of dark, wavy hair. The bastardized Oscar Wilde tag line is prophetic: "Be yourself, everyone else is already taken". I feel like I've vanished from my neck down.

It's probably a re-pinned stock photo, not an actual photo of her. Her pin board shows we're into the same bands and the same food. If I weren't so freaked out, I might copy down some of her recipes. There's a Lebanese chick pea and sweet potato dish Da– Dr Tyler would really like. I hold my breath for seventeen seconds. Either Mom has the mentality of a

GIRL, WORLD

teenage girl or Mom has a namesake offspring. The bottoms of my feet start to itch.

I need a dose of Fico.

I'm standing at the kitchen patio door, red velvet cupcakes in hand, when he arrives.

'I got your text.' His eyes are fixed to my cakes.

'I should make these into a bra.'

Fico's nose wrinkles like he smells feet. 'It'd be a look.' His index finger is nail deep in frosting before he has cleared the threshold. 'How's life as an *X-Men*?'

'Lonely.'

Fico breaks into "All By Myself" until I yank his air microphone away.

'So, I've been looking for my mom and I found something-ish.' My laptop is open to Danica Babic's Pinterest board.

'So?'

'So maybe this is my mother or my sister.'

'Could be. Didn't your Dad–'

'Uh-uh. My Franken-creator.'

Fico rolls his eyes. 'Didn't your Franken-creator say your mom had her own plans? If she'd worked hard to get a scholarship here, I don't think she'd have thrown it all away to go to Serbia.'

'I don't believe anything he says. When I find my mom, I'm going to ask if I can stay with her for a while. I have these rotating fantasies of meeting her. In one, she wants to know what my favorite dessert is so she can make it. She starts a food fight and we're covered in flour, laughing. We end up making it together. In another, she takes me to some smoky Art Deco café. We're both wearing blond wigs, classy, and white gloves. Over champagne cocktails, she tells me what

ALEX POPPE

Dr Tyler was like when he had a heart. In another version, we go somewhere quiet and cultured where she teaches me dirty limericks so I laugh out loud at inappropriate times. We always stay up until the sun rises, and then she sings one of her grandmother's Serbian lullabies as I fall asleep in her bed.'

'Take a huge bite of cupcake please.'

'I don't want any.'

'Just do it.'

'Why?'

'Do it. More. More. And some more please. Don't swallow.'

Almost the whole cupcake is in my mouth and I need to cough.

'I don't want you to yell at me when I say this next bit. You can't decide that your mom was right and Dr Tyler was wrong because people are different things at the same time. You can swallow now.'

My teeth hurt from the icing. 'It sounds like you're taking his side.'

'I'm on your side. But you're acting like a Lifetime Movie Network special. You're building this mother-story up in your head, inventing bonding moments. You've probably already cast her. But your mom is a stranger to you. She left. Dr Tyler took care of you. Maybe he did it for research and maybe he didn't. It could have been a bit of both. Does it matter?'

'Yes. He pretended to love me and all that time, he was probably laughing behind my back at how stupid I was to believe it.'

'Why do you think he was pretending? He could have done a lot less if you were just his mad science project.'

I get up to get us both some milk. 'It doesn't make it right.'

'And where do you get him laughing from? He's always proud of you.'

GIRL, WORLD

'Proud of his creation.'

'Same thing.'

Fico has a point. We clink glasses and both take a long swallow of milk. 'So Marie watches Lifetime?'

'Sometimes.'

'Milla Jovovich, as long as we're sharing.'

'As your mother? She can't act.'

'But, little known fact, she can sing. Plus, her boobs are a tasteful size.'

'She has great style. I'll give her that.' Fico drains his milk and studies the bottom of the glass. 'You're setting yourself up for disappointment.'

'I know.' I laugh in spite of myself. Fico's milk mustache more than hints at The Joker.

'What?'

'Nice stash.'

'You too.'

We whip out our cell phones to selfie the moment as Dr Tyler enters the kitchen.

'Hello Fico. It's been a while.'

'Hello Dr Tyler. Yeah, I'm in rehearsals for *Rent*.'

No one says anything for several seconds until Fico's elbow connects to my ribs. 'Hello Dr Tyler.' I mimic Fico.

'Hello Nastasia. How was school?'

'Fine.'

Another thundering silence. It seems as if the three of us have been transported inside Homer Simpson's head. I imagine tumbleweeds blowing across swaths of arid land.

'So,' Fico stands. 'I should probably go.'

'Why don't you stay for dinner?' I stand too.

'Because this is really uncomfortable.' He looks from Dr Tyler to me. 'Sorry.'

ALEX POPPE

'No doubt Nastasia has told you of her recent findings.'
'He knows about my triple X chromosomes.'
'Fico, if it isn't too much trouble, I am curious to hear your opinion.'
'I'm sorry, sir. I don't have one.'
Sir? Who is Fico kidding? 'Daresay young chap, I agree with Dr Tyler. I, too, would find your viewpoint quite piquant.' I channel my inner Katherine Hepburn.
Dr Tyler and I move a little closer to Fico. He has no escape.
'I think your superpowers are cool and I wish I had them too. But I wouldn't want to be the subject of a research experiment. Also, I would have wanted to know the truth sooner. And I very much want to leave now.' Fico practically runs from the house.
'Well done. I hope you're satisfied.' I carry our glasses to the sink.
'I am. He wishes he had your advantages.'
'He also thinks you lied to me and used me.'
'He didn't say that.'
'I don't care. *I* wish you hadn't lied to me and used me. And I'm the one who counts.'
'Nastasia, I am sorry I didn't tell you and you had to find out the way you did. I hope one day you will forgive me.' He touches my shoulder with an envelope.
'Brave envelope.'
'Open it.'
'It better contain backstage passes to the next Beyoncé concert. Clemency costs.'
'You'll like this too.'
Inside is the contact information for one Danica Babic, of Kreuzberg, Berlin. I'm speechless. I never thought he'd

GIRL, WORLD

help. There are also two plane tickets. It's a shameless bribe, but I fall for it.

'What do you think?' He truly asks. Instead of looking proud of himself, his smile is wrinkled.

'Better than Beyoncé.'

'I'd like to accompany you, but if not, I'll arrange for someone to take you.'

'You can come.' Small mercies. I know he wants to see her too. 'Do you think we should contact her first or ambush her?' I can't believe this is really happening.

'I'll leave that up to you.' He heads upstairs.

'Dr Tyler, D-Dad,' that word feels foreign in my mouth. 'How did–'

'Your old man still has a few tricks up his sleeve.' He calls from the upstairs landing. 'How about Thai for dinner?'

I can't tell who's playing whom.

❖

There are faces on the facades. Mostly lions, but some girl faces too, chiseled into the majestic stone. Tons of graffiti – cartoon men in shirt ties and chained handcuffs, little naked monster men swarming a giant naked monster man, a two-storey high portrait of a man's face chiseled into a plaster-covered brick wall – adorn the buildings, turning the city into an open air gallery. Alack, alas, so many men, so little time. I have a mother to find.

Bright chips of sunlight rearrange themselves on the grass as we cut through an arty trailer park near the River Spree. The eau de marijuana wafting through the trees probably has nothing to do with tall, skinny dudes in Rasta garb patrolling the park's entrance. We ignore the cat calls. Their

ALEX POPPE

eyes follow us as my vanilla escort takes my hand and leads me down a narrow stone path. Dad's palm is sweaty. The path burps us out into a gentrifying neighborhood. Almost every other store front is a café or eatery.

We stand outside Balkanika, a gourmet delicatessen slash wine bar. A ginormous deli case containing dips, spreads, borek, and stuffed grape leaves cajoles us through a glass window. Dad must be in anticipatory hummus heaven.

'This is it.' Dad smiles the type of smile people have when they wonder if their hair is out of place. 'Ready?'

'Ready.' I am anything but. Pop rockets are going off in my stomach. A tinkering bell announces our entrance. No one is behind the counter.

'Nastasia, look.' Dad points to a display of jars containing gourmet jam made of fig and cocoa inside a wooden crate. The brand name is Ficoco.

'I can't believe it. Let me take a picture. We have to get him some.' This makes Fico an ASS, an actor/singer/ sandwich spread.

Dad takes a jar and turns toward the window to read its label. 'It's made in Croatia.' His back is toward me when a slender woman with dark curly hair enters from some back storeroom wearing a black, silky slip dress. Her wide smile balances her high forehead and strong nose. Her dress clings to her amazing, gorgeous breasts. They are perfect. There is nothing more to say.

CPSIA information can be obtained
at www.ICGtesting.com
Printed in the USA
BVHW07s1111110618
518747BV00022B/1235/P